Beyond

the

Dare

By Hayzel Greene

Copyright

Dedication

In loving memory of:

Linda Taylor Fisher "Jeannie" – who always told me I was close to being a genius, and that if I put my mind to it, it could be done.

Willie Demetrius Jones "Bleu" – who showed me life on the other side of the fence.

April Monique Mitchell "Appprreeelll" – who proved that after the tears, there can still be laughter.

Temujin Monroe Hood "P'Nut" – who showed me what true friendship really means.

Charles Taylor "Chawyas Tay" – who taught me the true spirit of a Hip-Hop Head. **Awl Fuckit' Chawles**

You are all a part of me,
and through every word I write,
your voices live on.

I dedicate these words in this book to you all for believing in me, pouring into me, and being a part of my journey.

Acknowledgments

I dedicate these words to everyone who has ever believed in me, poured into me, and walked with me on this journey.

First and foremost, to my mother, **Linda Taylor Fisher** — your love, wisdom, and strength continue to guide me in ways words can't fully capture. Every page I write carries a piece of you.

To my two beautiful daughters — you are my light and my reason. May you always know your dreams are worth chasing and your voices deserve to be heard.

To my friends who left this world too soon — **April, Bleu, and Temujin** — your laughter, encouragement, and belief in me live on in my heart. This book, and every story that follows, carries your spirit between its lines.

To the ones still walking this journey beside me — **Tanya "TNic" Anderson, LeDawn "Shy Sistah" Hardnick, and MBoss** — thank you for your strength, your laughter, and your constant reminders that art, like love, takes community.

To every reader, supporter, and believer in **The HG Collection** — thank you for reminding me that stories have power when they come from a place of truth.

You have all taught me resilience, reminded me of love's reach, and helped me keep creating when the noise got too loud.

Beyond the Dare is not just my story — it is a reflection of every lesson, laughter, and memory stitched into this journey. — **Hayzel Greene**

Beyond the Dare

Preface

Beyond the Dare started as a short story, one of many I wrote during a time when imagination was my refuge and writing was my therapy. What began as a playful 'what if' turned into something much bigger: a journey of love, redemption, trust, and the courage to move past heartbreak into something greater.

This story isn't just about two people rekindling a connection from the past—it's about how we dare ourselves to heal, to open our hearts again, and to believe in love even after it has hurt us.

I wrote this book for anyone who has ever questioned whether they are enough, for anyone who has stood at the edge of doubt and wondered if they can leap again.

Hope that *Beyond the Dare* inspires you to see your own resilience, to embrace the unexpected, and to know that real, steady, lasting love—is worth fighting for.

Thank you for daring to take this journey with me.

— *Hayzel Greene*

Table of Contents

Copyright .... *i*

Dedication .... *iii*

Acknowledgments .... *iv*

Preface .... *v*

Table of Contents .... *vi*

Chapters

• Chapter 1 — Dana 1

• Chapter 2 — Dana & Antwon 7

• Chapter 3 — Antwon 15

• Chapter 4 — Dana 21

• Chapter 5 — Antwon 25

• Chapter 6 — Dana 31

• Chapter 7 — Antwon 37

• Chapter 8 — Dana 39

• Chapter 9 — Antwon 43

• Chapter 10 — Dana 47

• Chapter 11 — Antwon 53

• Chapter 12 — Dana 57

• Chapter 13 — Antwon 61

• Chapter 14 — Dana 63

• Chapter 15 — Antwon 69

• Chapter 16 — Dana 71

• Chapter 17 — Antwon 73

• Chapter 18 — Dana 79

Hayzel Greene

- Chapter 19 — Antwon 85
- Chapter 20 — Dana 89
- Chapter 21 — Antwon 91
- Chapter 22 — Antwon 95
- Chapter 23 — Dana 99
- Chapter 24 — Antwon 105
- Chapter 25 — Dana 111
- Chapter 26 — Antwon 115
- Chapter 27 — Antwon 119
- Chapter 28 — Dana 123
- Chapter 29 — Antwon 125

Epilogues

- Epilogue I — Full Circle 129
- Epilogue II — The Future 131

Back Matter

- About the Author — Hayzel Greene 133
- Other Works by Hayzel Greene 134
- Coming Soon 135

Hayzel Greene

Chapter 1 – Dana

It had been too long since I'd kicked it with my girls. Life pulled us in different directions, distance stretched our antics thin—but somehow, the friendship held. This reunion was overdue. Just knowing we'd be in the same room again felt like a celebration.

Four years had passed since our last dare in Vegas. We still laughed about it over the phone, but talking about it wasn't the same as reliving it side by side. Another reason I couldn't miss my goddaughter's birthday party.

Ladies, here I come.

Friday before a holiday weekend meant airport chaos. The line at the ticket counter dragged, TSA was worse, and by the time I reached the gate, I was drained. I spotted a window seat and slid into it, clutching my carry-on like it held my sanity.

The couple from earlier—Mr. and Mrs. Evans, honeymooning on a vow renewal—sat across the aisle. Sweet, too sweet. Their PDA had me half-smiling, half-nauseous. I congratulated them politely, then shoved in my earbuds and drowned myself in my audiobook until their flight was called. Relief washed over me as they disappeared into the boarding line.

I closed my eyes, letting the narrator's voice smooth my edges—until the cushion beside me dipped.

A young guy in basketball shorts and a hoodie dropped into the seat. I offered a polite nod, slid back into my book, and tried to ignore him. When I glanced up again, the hoodie was gone. In his place sat a man who made the air in my chest catch.

Chocolate skin. Broad shoulders. The kind of presence you felt before your eyes caught up.

Antwon

Four years vanished in a blink. I remembered him. Every detail. Every. Single. Inch.

My pulse spiked. Not just from memory—the kind of memory that leaves your skin tingling—but from the ache that came with it. Because after all that heat, all that connection, all that dare… he never called.

Damn, he still looked good. But forget that. He didn't even call.

His gaze lingered on me, narrowing slightly, like he was trying to place me. Panic flared. Don't tell me he doesn't remember.

I dropped my eyes on my phone, scrolling through nothing, praying he'd stay quiet.

"Hello." His baritone slid into me, smooth and familiar.

I stiffened, then forced a short reply. "Hey."

"How are you doing?"

"Fine." (beat) "You?"

"Can't complain." That smile was still lethal. "Funny running into you here."

Funny? I almost laughed out loud. Four years and one unanswered number later, *funny* wasn't the word.

"Running into people tends to go nowhere," I muttered, eyes on my phone.

He let it slide. "So… how've you been?"

I looked up, sharp. "Guess it wasn't long enough. You didn't call."

That hit. His smirk faded.

"You're right," he said slowly. "I should have. Truth is… I couldn't."

I arched a brow. "Couldn't, wouldn't, or didn't?"

"Couldn't." He leaned closer, steady eyes locked on mine. "I dropped my phone in the tub the next day. Had to replace it. Your number wasn't saved. Just like that, it was gone."

My arms folded tight. It sounded like an excuse. Probably was. But the way his gaze didn't waver made me want to believe it and that unsettled me most of all.

"You wouldn't believe what I went through to find you," he added.

"You looked?"

"Yeah. For years. And when I thought there would be no hope, and that I should just chalk it up as a wonderful memory, I ran into your friend

Danielle at the courthouse, of all places. As she reminded me of where I knew her from, I asked about you. She looked at me as if I were weird, but I had to know. Why not ask and see if I could get any answers."

My throat tightened. The way he said it… the way his voice wrapped around me like heat…

Before I could stop myself, memories surged. Vegas. That night. The dare I never should've taken.

~~~~~

It was supposed to be harmless. One last hurrah. Danielle had smirked at me, drink in hand, and said, *"Last dares on you, Dana. Find a man, make it count. Pictures for proof."*

I'd scanned the bar and landed on him. Antwon. Broad shoulders hunched, drink cradled like it carried his worries. He looked like someone waiting for the right woman to sit down and change his night.

So, I did.

Hello, I'd said, sliding onto the stool beside him.

Hello, he answered, velvet-voiced.

One drink became two, teasing banter flowed, and before I knew it, we were at the buffet at midnight, laughing over coffee. He told me that he graduated with a degree in Criminal Justice and living beyond his family's expectations. I let him see parts of me I didn't share with most men—my dreams, my edges, the unpolished truths.

Hayzel Greene

And when the night blurred hotter, when his hands were on my skin and his mouth traced every part of me, it didn't feel like a game anymore. No dare had ever felt like that.

~~~~~

"Alright," I said now, steadying my breath, pulling myself back into the present. "Let's talk before the plane boards. I need to know why you're here."

He leaned forward, elbows on his knees. "Fair enough. Let's get to know each other. Properly this time."

His words sank into me, quickening my pulse.

Minutes later, I boarded, only to be stopped mid-aisle. *Upgrade.* The attendant smiled, guiding me to the seat next to him.

"You didn't have to," I whispered.

"Please," he said smoothly, settling in. "I insist. How else can we finish?"

Through takeoff and into the air, conversation ran easily, charged with something unspoken. He told me about the bar he co-owned with his cousin, and how his degree gave him a business edge. I shared pieces of my past too—my lessons, heartbreaks, how independence sometimes felt like armor.

Our glances lingered. Slight touches found themselves on another. The sunset outside painted gold across the clouds, and the air between us thickened.

Touchdown came too soon. At baggage claim, we walked close, stealing glances, his laughter softening my clumsy run-in with a woman's walker.

The Uber ride pulsed with quiet sparks. When our hands brushed, I swore the driver could feel the static too.

At my stop, I turned. "Give me your phone."

He didn't hesitate. Unlocked it, handed it over. Trust, just like that.

I dialed, let my number flash across his screen, then killed the call before it connected. I gave it back with a smile. "Not leaving this to chance."

His gaze burned into me as I stepped out, heat clinging to my skin.

Back at my hotel, I tried to focus on tomorrow's party, the reunion. But when my phone buzzed, my heart already knew.

Still thinking about you, that night, and our rekindling.

Warmth flooded me. My reply came fast. *Same here.*

The glow of the screen faded, but sleep didn't come easy. His dimples, his touch, his eyes followed me.

And under it all, one thought refused to quiet:

What if giving him another chance meant losing myself all over again?

Chapter 2 – Dana & Antwon

The morning light pushed through the curtains, soft and golden, dragging me out of the half-sleep I'd managed. My body was still reacting from Antwon's text, from the memory of his eyes, his voice, his touch. Tossing and turning all night hadn't put him away.

I stretched, shook it off. Today wasn't about him. It was about my girls, my goddaughter, and my family.

I had one leg in my jeans when a knock rattled the door.

I froze. Nobody knew what room I was in. Not my girls. Definitely not Antwon.

Another knock.

I cracked it open. Room service. A cart rolled in with breakfast for one, and roses. Long-stemmed, proud, red.

My throat closed.

"Compliments of a friend," the server said, smiling before slipping out.

A friend. Yeah, right.

Heat coiled in my stomach before I could stop it. My body remembered too much on how his hands once mapped every inch of me, how his voice had unraveled me like I'd been waiting for him all my life.

His gesture was sweet. Too sweet. A little too sweet where I had doubt in his sincerity.

My phone buzzed on the nightstand.

Good morning, beautiful. Hope you enjoy breakfast. Have a wonderful time with your girls today.

A smile tugged at my lips, traitorous and uninvited. He knew exactly how to slip under my skin. Exactly how to make me remember.

I set the phone face down, like that could block him out. Today wasn't his. Today was mine.

Still, as I poured the coffee, the scent rising warm and rich, his words lingered like heat in my chest.

~~~~~

The Uber ride felt too short, like the streets were rushing me. By the time we pulled up in front of Sam's brick two-story, laughter and music drifted out from the backyard.

The gate was open, voices carrying like a welcome mat. I stepped through and into the noise, the chaos, the love.

Sam at the grill, Danielle tying balloons, Lani scrolling while her daughter braided doll hair.

"Look who finally showed up!" Sam hollered, waving tongs like a sword.

"Bout time!" Danielle grinned, arms wide.

Hayzel Greene

Hugs smothered me, kids tugged at my hands, laughter wrapped me up until—for a moment—I almost forgot about Antwon. Almost.

The backyard buzzed with life: balloons bobbing, smoke rising from the grill, sheet cake sparkling with sprinkles. My goddaughter spotted me and came barreling, tiara crooked on her head.

"Auntie Dana!"

I scooped her up and kissed her cheek. "Happy birthday, baby girl."

From my bag, I pulled out the gift: a pink karaoke machine. Her eyes went wide; her squeal shook the yard.

The party blurred—candles, frosting, kids rapping off-key to 50 Cent like a backyard concert. We adults laughed, refereed, and eventually collapsed into chairs with wine and spiked punch like queens after battle.

"This," Danielle sighed, sipping, "is the part I live for."

We clinked glasses, traded updates, until the lull hit. And then came the look. The shift.

"So…" Lani leaned in, eyebrow arched. "Word is, you had a little visitor?"

I shot Danielle a glare.

"Okay, okay," she said with a guilty grin. "I may have slipped him the info. Didn't think he'd show."

"Who?" Lani pressed. Being new to the group she was not privy to our Vegas trip.

"Antwon," I said flatly.

Sam's glass nearly tipped. "Vegas Antwon? Mr. Chocolatey himself?"

"Mr. Ouchie Wally," Danielle added, biting her lip.

I groaned. "Yes. That Antwon."

"And?" Danielle pushed.

"And nothing. He showed up, talked about the past, and said he wanted to see me again."

Sam leaned forward. "So, what's the problem?"

My throat tightened. Eddie's name burned at the back of my mind.

"The problem is," I said slowly, "the last time I let my guard down, I ended up wrecked."

Danielle frowned. "Eddie?"

I nodded. "Walked in and he was with somebody else. Didn't even flinch."

Sam cursed under her breath. Lani shook her head. Danielle reached for my hand.

"Fuck Eddie," she said softly. "That was him, not you. Don't let his bullshit keep you from something real."

Their words sat heavy, warming and hurting at the same time. I leaned back, watching the pink sky fade.

"Antwon moved me to first class yesterday," I admitted.

Three heads snapped toward me.

"What?" Danielle gasped.

"Upgraded my seat on the plane and sent breakfast and roses to my room this morning."

Sam whistled low. "That's not just a move. That's effort."

Danielle smirked. "Eddie never brought you roses."

I laughed, thin and shaky. "That's the problem. It feels good—too good. And I don't know if I can trust it."

Sam sipped slowly. "You don't have to trust it yet. Just… see what happens."

The thought settled, dangerous and tempting. Could I?

Antwon

The hotel room was too damn quiet.

I'd been up since before sunrise, pacing. I wasn't the kind of man who sent roses and breakfast trays, but with Dana… it felt right. Vegas had been years ago, but I remembered how she loved coffee in the morning, how she laughed when flowers filled the lobby at Caesars. Trivial things. Things a man doesn't forget when a woman gets under his skin.

The roses weren't about romance. They were proof—I remembered.

But proof wasn't enough. Not after four years of silence.

I typed out three texts and deleted them before landing on the one I sent. **Good morning, beautiful.** Simple. Careful. Enough to tell her I was thinking of her, but not so much that it felt like pressure.

Now I sat on the edge of the bed, restlessly, staring at my phone like it might conjure her reply. Nothing.

I thought about showing up at Sam's. I knew that is where she was headed. Danielle had told me, half by accident, half because I pressed. But barging in would have been too much, too soon.

Instead, I stayed put, forcing myself to have patience.

Vegas replayed in my mind like a movie I couldn't turn off, her laugh at the buffet, the way she opened about dreams she hadn't told her friends, the way her eyes locked on mine like she was daring me to hold her tighter.

I had not forgotten one thing.

And when I almost lost that number? I swore if I ever got another chance, I would not waste it.

So, I waited, restless, staring at the roses on her tray in my imagination, picturing her face when she saw them.

I wanted her to smile. I wanted her to curse me out. I wanted her to feel something, anything—but indifference.

My phone stayed silent. I rubbed my hand over my jaw, exhaled hard.

I was not going to chase her down today. Not when she deserved her girls, her family, her peace.

Hayzel Greene

But the truth settled like fire in my chest:

I'm not letting her slip away again.

Beyond the Dare

Chapter 3 – Antwon

The courtroom buzzed with quiet chatter, but my mind was sharp, locked in. Opposing counsel droned on, waving papers like smoke and mirrors, but I could tell the jury wasn't buying it.

I've been here before. This was the dance I trained for, the objections, the cross, the rhythm of trial. And I wasn't about to lose.

When it was my turn, I stood, buttoned my jacket, and laid out the facts clean, simple, and undeniable. No theatrics, no grand speeches, just precision.

By the time I sat back down, the energy had shifted. Case closed.

The verdict came in our favor. My client hugged me, tears soaking my shoulder. That rush—that satisfaction of doing it right—never got old.

Outside the courtroom, I was sliding files into my briefcase when a woman stepped into my path.

"Excuse me… you look familiar. Is your name Antwon?"

"Yes," I said cautiously. "Do I know you?"

She chuckled. "Not exactly. But I know you. Four years ago—Vegas."

I frowned, studying her. Then she gave me the name that cut straight through.

"Dana."

The air shifted.

Pieces clicked. I remembered flashes—her in the background that night, her laugh floating across the room. Dana's friend.

"Danielle," she said, extending a hand. "Trust me—back then, you and Dana had everybody's attention."

I straightened. "What are you doing here?"

"Court date. Caught up in a lawsuit. Watching you in there today… I wish my lawyer had half your sense."

"Tell me what's going on," I said.

She laid it out fast, and I pointed out a couple of things her attorney had missed. Her shoulders eased instantly.

"How much do I owe you for that?" she asked.

"Connect me with Dana. That's payment enough."

Her smile froze. "Still stuck on her, huh?"

"Not stuck. Unfinished."

Danielle studied for a long moment, then sighed. "Alright. Since you just saved me a fortune… I guess it won't hurt to tell you. She will be going to our goddaughter's birthday party in Georgia.

"Which part of Georgia?" I asked.

"Columbus, Columbus, Georgia. She should be leaving from Hopkins next Saturday on the 3:30 flight. That's all I've got."

Hayzel Greene

It was enough. More than enough.

~~~~~

Daytime Parallel

I wasn't built to sit around waiting. Even with Dana running through my mind, I had to move.

I told myself I needed a new tie, so I ducked into a men's store downtown. But my feet carried me into the women's section. A red dress on a mannequin stopped me cold—sleek lines, soft fabric that made me picture Dana filling it out in all the right places.

I didn't buy it. Too soon. But I stood there longer than I should have, fighting the urge.

Back outside, I checked in with the bar. I was assured that everyone was at work, no call-offs; all the shelves were stocked, and the weekend was steady. Business never stopped, not even when my head was somewhere else.

Then I scrolled to a name I hadn't called in a while—my cousin Dre. He was one of the ones who never let me forget Dana, clowning me every year about "the girl in Vegas."

When he picked up, his laugh hit my ear. "What's good, man?"

"You ain't gonna believe this," I said. "I found her."

Silence, then: "Quit playing."

"Dead serious. Seeing her yesterday. Sat with her on the plane. Even got her number again."

Dre whistled low. "So, what's the move?"

"That's the problem. She's guarded. Some fool named Eddie did her dirty. I can feel it in the way she talks, like she's bracing for the next hit."

Dre chuckled. "Bruh, you've been talking about her for years. If anybody's gonna wait this out, it's you."

"Patience isn't my strong suit," I muttered.

"Then learn. She's worth it."

We talked a little longer before I hung up. Saying it out loud made my chest feel lighter.

~~~~~

Night Text

I told myself I wouldn't text her again tonight. She needed space, not pressure.

But at ten o'clock, my phone lit up.

Made it back to the hotel. Long day.

I stared at the words, a slow grin tugging at my mouth. She reached out first. That wasn't small talk, it was an opening.

Glad you got in safely. Did you have an enjoyable time? I typed.

There was a pause. Three dots. Disappeared. Came back again. Finally:

Hayzel Greene

Yeah, the kids wore us out. But it was good catching up. Relaxing now.

I pictured her stretched across hotel sheets, hair down, glowing in the light of her phone.

Hope tomorrow's good to you, I sent, deleting the line I wanted to add—*Wish I was there.* Too soon.

Moments later: *What time are you heading back?*

My chest tightened. That was the door I had been waiting for.

Whenever you are. What is your flight?

She hesitated but eventually sent the details. I leaned back, smiling in the dark.

She did not know it yet, but I'd already made my choice.

If Dana were leaving tomorrow, I'd be on that plane too.

Beyond the Dare

Chapter 4 – Dana

Morning was evident. The sunlight spilled across the bed, dragging me into my reality. I lay there looking at the ceiling, my body rested but my mind restless. Time to go home.

My phone vibrated. Danielle.

"Morning, sleepyhead. Hold on—let me bring Sam in."

Seconds later, Sam's voice chimed through the speaker. "Morning, sunshine."

"Morning," I mumbled, stretching.

Danielle laughed. "Don't sound too excited. You packed yet?"

"Almost," I said. "Flight's later this morning."

They wished me safe travels, but I should've known they wouldn't let me off easily.

"So," Sam drawled. "Did you talk back to Antwon?"

As if on cue, my phone buzzed with a new message. I glanced down.

Good morning. Before the flight, let me take you to breakfast. I can send a car at 9am if that is okay with you. No pressure, just food and conversation.

"He just invited me to breakfast," I said, trying to keep my voice neutral but failing.

Sam's laugh burst through the phone. "Girl, go! Eat the food, drink the coffee, and don't overthink it."

Danielle's tone softened. "Just… be open. That's all."

I hesitated only a second before typing back: *Okay.*

We said our goodbyes and hung up, and I practically leapt into the shower. By the time I finished packing, my pulse was a steady drum.

The car was sleek and black, waiting at the curb. The driver greeted me by name and took my bag. The whole thing felt deliberate. Considered. Him.

Antwon was waiting in the lobby, crisp shirt, slacks, smile warm but careful.

"Good morning," he said.

"Morning."

The table was tucked in a quiet corner near the window. I can tell he had chosen that space on purpose, I could tell. Breakfast for the two of us, a space just for the two of us.

We talked while we sipped and ate. He mentioned cases that he could, the ones that had kept him in court all week, the kind of work that demanded all his attention. I admitted deadlines stacked on my desk were waiting for the second I landed. It should've been casual, small talk. But the way his eyes stayed on me—like he was taking in every word—made it feel like something else.

"So, you've always been in Ohio?" I asked.

Hayzel Greene

"About thirty minutes down the freeway from you," he said, smirking just enough. "Close enough to show up. Far enough not to crowd you."

I laughed, but the heat behind his words tugged at me.

Time slipped faster than I wanted. Too soon, he called for a car, and together we slid into the backseat.

At the terminal, he pulled me into a hug—firm, steady—and pressed a soft kiss to my cheek. Not rushed. Not casual. A promise wrapped in restraint.

We were on different flights, but when he whispered, *see you later,* I melted. Heat pooled low in my belly, that familiar ache reminding me exactly how much power his touch still had.

And as I walked away, my heart caught between two truths:
I wasn't ready to let him back in… but God, I wasn't ready to let him go either.

Beyond the Dare

Chapter 5 – Antwon

By nine a.m., my head was swimming in motions and exhibits—but my hands were ordering flowers.

Court always sharpens me. I like the ritual of it: the jacket buttoned, the table set, the quiet moment before everyone filing in and pretending we aren't about to wage a polite war. Today's skirmish was a pre-trial conference—tight timelines, one judge who hated theatrics and loved receipts. My lane.

We wrapped the first matter in under thirty minutes. Clean. Precise. The kind of win that doesn't make headlines but moves lives forward. On the way out, opposing counsel tried small talk; I gave him a nod and kept moving. My phone buzzed. Staff ping about the bar—delivery window changed for tonight. I shot back instructions and a quick "stack top-shelf left, mixers right; rotate stock."

Then I hit the florist.

"Same roses as yesterday," I said, "but give me a slimmer profile. Elegant. I don't want to look like I'm apologizing. This is… presence."

"Yes, sir. Card?"

I pictured Dana at her desk, headphones on, a room full of voices orbiting her while she solved three problems at once. I wanted the bouquet to land like a breath—noticeable, not noisy.

"Write: To break up the monotony… enjoy your day. Thoughts of you are fresh. —A."

I gave the delivery address—not her direct line, but reception. Let it sit where people pass, a question mark with a ribbon.

The rest of the morning, I worked. Drafts, calls, a witness prep that went from shaky to solid when I reframed the timeline like a highway: mile markers, exits, no detours. At lunch, I ate standing up in the chambers' hallway, texting the bar manager a reminder about ID checks—Friday nights bring tourists with baby faces and bold lies.

Around two, a thought came and went: *Has she seen them yet?* I kept my hands off my phone. Because that was the point. No pressure. Just a soft interruption in her day that didn't ask for anything back.

Late afternoon, the courthouse thinned. I walked outside into pale sun and cool air, loosened my tie, and let the city noise rinse the trial rhythm out of my head. Dre called.

"Quarterback," he said, laughing at the hello. "What's the score?"

"Up at the half," I said. "Flowers delivered to the fifty."

He whooped. "She texted yet?"

"Not yet."

"You sweating it?"

I smiled. "No. I'm letting time do work."

He sat quietly looking at me as if he had something on his mind.

Hayzel Greene

"You got patience now?"

"I got intention," I said. "Different thing."

We hung up. Saying it out loud made it real—that this wasn't a chase anymore. It was something deliberate.

Twilight stretched. I skimmed a brief, then re-read a line that made the whole argument click. I drafted a paragraph that felt like a key turning in a lock.

My phone buzzed.

Dana: *Flowers landed. You made me the talk of the office. Thank you.*

I let the message sit one full breath—respect, not strategy. Then:

Me: *Guilty of breaking monotony. I'll accept the sentence if it includes your smile.*

Three dots. They vanished. Came back.

Dana: *Consider it time served.*

I laughed, alone in my office, like a man who just won something nobody else could see.

I typed, deleted, typed again.

Me: *Two highlights, one headache—want to trade? I'll start.*

I sent a clean version of my day—no swagger. *Highlight: the judge bought our timeline. Second: witness finally solid. Headache: bar delivery tried to cut me at the knees.*

Three dots. Then:

Dana: *Highlight: sprint plan done. Second: got a blocker cleared without a meeting (miracle). Headache: someone microwaved fish. Again.*

Me: *Crimes against humanity. I'll draft a motion.*

She sent a laughing emoji. Then, a quiet line:

Dana: *Card was… thoughtful. "Fresh." That word stuck.*

Her words hit harder than she knew. Proof I was getting through. **This time, I wasn't letting her slip away into memory.**

Me: *It felt true.*

We fell into a pause that did not feel empty. The streetlights blinked outside; the city's motion continued. I could almost see her—bag at her feet, one heel kicked off under the desk, thumb hovering over the screen like she was lining up something careful.

Dana: *Tomorrows tight. If I go quiet, I'm just buried—not gone.*

There it was: trust, handed to me in a sentence.

Me: *Heard. I'll be on the same planet, different courtrooms. Knock out your day. I'll be here when you come up for air.*

I set the phone down and leaned back, letting the chair take my weight. The room felt wider. The week felt like possible. Vegas had been the spark; this was the wiring.

Before I left, I booked a table in her city for next week. Not a demand—an option. A note to myself that intention isn't noise; it's rhythm.

Hayzel Greene

When the confirmation email chimed, I pictured her bouquet at the reception desk, the way people would ask *Who?* and she'd tuck the card back into the leaves and keep walking, the secret warming her from the inside.

I turned off the light, stepped into the hallway, and let the door click shut behind me.

Tonight, I wouldn't chase. I didn't need to.

She'd already met me halfway.

Beyond the Dare

Chapter 6 – Dana

I arrived just before seven, nerves fluttering in my stomach like I was walking into an interview I hadn't prepared for. The host led me across the dining room, and there he was, Antwon. He was wearing a crisp navy jacket, open collar, posture steady and commanding like he owned the space without trying.

When his eyes landed on me, I froze. His gaze swept from my heels up to the fitted emerald dress that was hugging me just enough. All heat. No apology.

"You really know how to shut a room down," he said, rising as I approached.

The words curled low in my stomach. "Just figured I'd try to keep up," I teased, sliding into the chair across from him.

Dinner started light. He asked about my projects, and I found myself talking more than I expected deadlines, smoothing conflicts, the quiet pride in pulling chaos into order. He listened, not with polite nods, but with eyes locked on me, steady, attentive. Unnerving and addictive all at once.

I asked about his caseload, and he told a courtroom story that had me laughing into my wine. For a moment, it was easy—warm, charged, steady. Like maybe this wasn't impossible after all.

Then my laughter snapped short. My throat closed.

Because Eddie had just walked in. His hand wrapped around some woman's waist. His grin was as sharp as the knife he slid into my heart with his betrayal. They looked carefree, they were loud, like they were the entertainment that the restaurant paid for.

My fork stilled. Heat crawled up my neck. My shoulders locked. My chest hollowed out, shame and anger curling tight.

"Talk to me," Antwon said quietly, eyes narrowing as he followed my line of sight. "Who is that?"

"Eddie," I whispered, voice dry. "My ex, the one I told you about."

His expression shifted—calm, alert, and watchful. "You, okay?"

No. I was not. Not at the least. My pulse pounded in my ears. My body felt small, diminished, like Eddie had stolen the air from the room just by existing. "Yeah, I am good." But I really was not.

Just as Antwon was forming his lips to say more, Eddie saw me. And of course, he had to come over.

"Dana?" he said with a smirk, like we were old friends instead of wreckage. "Been a minute." He pulled the woman closer. "This is Sierra. Sierra, this is Dana."

I sat there and looked at him frozen. I was disgusted and I knew he could tell the way my face was tight. He was lucky my mouth didn't work; not for sure what I would have said.

Eddie's gaze slid to Antwon. "And you are?"

Hayzel Greene

Before I could answer, Antwon's hand slid over mine—firm, grounding. He rose, towering, voice smooth but edged in steel.

"Antwon Carrington," he said simply, extending a hand. His tone was polite, firm, and dismissive all at once; light he was saying you can go now.

Eddie's grin faltered under Antwon's grip. "Ah. Well. Nice to meet you."

"Likewise." Antwon's tone was polite, dismissive. A clear: you can go now.

Two minutes of shallow chatter followed—Eddie bragging, Antwon curt and professional. Finally, Eddie excused himself, tugging Sierra away. But not before glancing back, but a smug twist on his lips.

I exhaled hard, staring at my untouched plate, my body tight with leftover tremors.

Antwon leaned closer, voice low, meant only for me. "Look at me, Dana."

Reluctantly, my eyes lifted.

"He does not win just by existing. That chapter closed the day he betrayed you. You are sitting here with me. Right here, right now. And I am not him. You are the catch. I am glad he fucked up. Now, I can have you, all of you."

The words slipped into me, slow and steady, unraveling the knot Eddie had pulled tight. My chest loosened. My pulse steadied.

And for the first time all night I believed him.

The restaurant's hum pressed back in around us—clinking glasses, low laughter. I felt exposed, like everyone had seen me fold. But Antwon's hand was still covering mine, anchoring me.

Then he leaned back just slightly, enough to ease the mood. "So," he said lightly, "I still want to hear the end of that story about Sam and the karaoke mic."

A shaky laugh escaped. "She damn near snatched it out of the DJ's hand. The entire party stopped."

Antwon grinned. "I believe it."

The air softened again. The conversation drifted to safer waters. He told some funny stories, some memories, and glimpses of his work life. As I sat, the knot in my chest slowly loosened.

The server cleared the table and offered dessert; I shook my head. "I'm full."

He nodded. "Me too." Eyes set on me.

After leaving the restaurant, the cool night's air brushed my skin. The parking lot was quiet, half full and half-lit. His fingers brushed mine twice as he walked me to my car.

I was not sure why I didn't get my keys before we made it to the door. So, I fumbled through my purse, nerves buzzing with anxiety. He stood close shielding me from whatever as his presence wrapped me in heat.

"Call me and let me know you made it home," he said softly.

Hayzel Greene

I nodded instead of voicing my acknowledgement, my body lingered betraying me. My breath caught. The silence stretched for a few seconds longer, I stared at him not knowing what I wanted to do. My mind said grab him and dare him to kiss you, but reality said that was too forward of me. His hand brushed mine again, slower this time, deliberate.

My chest rose, suspended in the pause, as I stared at him until his lips found mine.

Or maybe mine found him. All I knew was the press of him, the way his hand cradled the back of my neck, steady and sure, and the way my body answered without hesitation.

His kiss deepened, long, unhurried. My fingers curled against his chest as his tongue teased mine, pulling a low ache from somewhere I thought I had buried.

When he finally drew back, both of us breathing heavy, his forehead rested against mine. Words hung unsaid, heavy between us.

"Drive safe," he whispered.

He opened my door, waited until I slid inside, then shut it gently. As I pulled away, I glanced back. He was still there—watching, hands in his pockets, jaw tight, eyes following until the night swallowed him whole.

By the time I parked, my hands were still trembling. I texted before I lost the nerve:

Made it home. Thank you for dinner. Thank you for being a perfect gentleman. And thank you… for saving me tonight.

Seconds later, his reply lit my screen:

Always. Sleep well, Dana.

Chapter 7 – Antwon

I couldn't get her out of my head. The kiss still burned on my lips, the warmth of her skin branded into my palm where I'd touched her cheek.

But every time the memory sweetened, Eddie's face cut through it. The way Dana's shoulders had locked, the way her voice had gone small when she saw him—it gnawed at me.

I hated that he still had that kind of power.

I dropped my jacket over the chair, loosened my tie, and poured a glass of water that I barely tasted. The townhouse was quiet, the kind of silence that made every thought louder. Outside, the city moved without me, headlights streaking against the curtains. But all I could hear was her voice, raw with hurt.

She deserved better than the shadows Eddie left behind.

And I wanted to be that better.

Not by sweeping her off her feet with flowers or fancy dinners—though God knows I wanted both. But by showing her, piece by piece, that I wasn't going anywhere. That I could hold space for her without crowding it.

Vegas had cracked something open in me. She didn't know it, but that night—her laugh over bad coffee, her body tangled with mine, the way she listened like every word mattered—it had made me believe anything was possible. I'd spent years trying to duplicate it with other women, but it was never the same. Not even close.

Because it wasn't just the sex, though the sex had been fire. It was her.

Now, she was back in my orbit. And time was short. Soon she would be buried in her routine again, walls rebuilt brick by brick. If I wanted this to be more than a memory, every move had to be intentional.

I set the glass down, rubbed the back of my neck, and made myself a quiet vow:

Dana would never feel "less" again. Not on my watch. Not with me.

Because I hadn't just come back to relive the past.
I'd come to rewrite the future.

Chapter 8 – Dana

Work had swallowed me whole again. Deadlines stacked high, emails firing faster than I could clear them, meetings that should've been emails. Same rhythm, different week.

But beneath it all, there was something new, someone new.

Antwon.

The kiss lingered on my lips even days later. Every time I replayed it, my chest squeezed, my thighs tightened, and I had to remind myself to breathe. The roses at my hotel had dried, but the memory hadn't. And the way he stood up to Eddie would be etched in stone.

So, when my phone buzzed around lunchtime, I almost ignored it. Until I saw his name.

Check the desk. Don't eat without me.

I frowned, confused. I'd packed leftovers. But when I walked out toward reception, there it was: a brown bag stamped with the logo from my favorite little café two blocks over. The receptionist grinned. "Somebody must really like you."

Heat rose in my cheeks as I carried the bag back. By the time I sat down, his FaceTime was ringing.

I answered, shaking my head with a smile. "Really?"

Antwon's face filled my screen, dimples flashing. "What? You told me once that their chicken salad sandwich saves your life on busy days. I listen."

I opened the bag. Sure enough, my usual order, right down to the iced tea. "You're ridiculous."

"Ridiculously thoughtful," he corrected. "Now eat with me." He tilted his phone to show his own spread—Chinese takeout cartons on his desk.

So, we ate. Chewed through stories, swapped bites on camera, and teased each other about who ate faster. It was silly, but it felt real—like we'd carved out our own little space in the middle of the chaos.

When the call ended, I leaned back in my chair, my chest warmer than it had been all week.

That evening, my phone buzzed again—this time with a group FaceTime. Danielle, Sam, and Lani's faces filled the screen like a panel of judges.

"Look at her," Sam said, sipping something from a wine glass. "She's glowing."

"Glowing?" I laughed, propping myself against my pillows. "I'm tired."

"Lies," Danielle cut in. "This is Antwon-glow."

Lani leaned closer to the screen. "So… you gonna update us, or are we dragging it out of you?"

I sighed, pretending exasperation, but my grin gave me away. "Fine. He kissed me."

Three voices shrieked at once.

Hayzel Greene

"Tell us everything!" Sam demanded.

"It was…" My voice trailed, and heat crept into my cheeks. "Long. Passionate. The kind you don't walk away from the same."

Danielle fanned herself dramatically. "Lord, have mercy."

I dropped my voice low, mimicking his calm tone: "Antwon Carrington."

The screen erupted Sam, almost spit out her drink, Danielle clapped like a seal, and Lani shook her head. "Girl, that gave me chills—and I wasn't even there."

We laughed until my sides hurt. Then I sobered a little. "Eddie was there that night. Walked in with a woman. He said her name was Sierra. I froze. I felt so small, like he still owned a piece of me just by existing."

The others went quietly. I pressed on. "But Antwon… he stood up. Took my hand. Introduced himself with a calm and steady demeaner. Not a flex. Just letting it be known that I was with him. It saved me the embarrassment."

"That's what we're talking about," Danielle said firmly. "Eddie doesn't get to keep you prisoner. Antwon showed you that."

Sam leaned in. "Plus, flowers at work? FaceTime lunch? Girl, he's consistent."

Lani smirked. "Not the corporate romance package."

We all cracked up again, but my chest was full. Warm. Settled.

Finally, Danielle leaned back with a knowing look. "You know if I hadn't dared you in Vegas, none of this would've happened, right? You wouldn't even *know* Antwon."

Sam and Lani chimed in at once. "Facts."

I rolled my eyes but couldn't hide my smile. "Yeah, yeah. I guess I owe you."

Danielle winked. "No guesses. You owe me big."

We laughed again, but the words stuck with me long after the call ended.

I set my phone down, stared at the empty sandwich wrapper, and whispered to myself:
"I think… I'm ready. To open myself up. To take his advances. To see where this could go."

For the first time in a long time, the idea of letting someone in didn't feel like a risk.

It felt like possibility.

Chapter 9 – Antwon

By ten a.m., my head was buried in motions and exhibits—but my thoughts were still with Dana.

I should've been outlining closing arguments, prepping for a deposition later in the week, but my mind kept circling back to her laugh on FaceTime, fork paused mid-air, eyes soft and unguarded. It felt too natural, too easy. Like we'd been doing this for years instead of days.

And that unsettled me, in the best way.

"Man, you got that look."

Dre leaned against my doorway, grinning. Didn't knock never did.

"What look?" I muttered, flipping a page for show.

"The look of a man who's sprung." He started crooning T-Pain's *I'm Sprung* until I flipped him off. Then he slid into Monica's *So Gone*, laughing loud enough to shake the walls.

"Why are you smiling at your paperwork like it just kissed you back?"

I smirked, throwing a pen cap at him. "Get outta my office." But he wasn't wrong. "It's just… different with her. Always has been. Even back in Vegas."

"Different how? You've had women lined up since college."

I stared at the diploma on my wall but saw her face instead. "With her, it ain't about filling time. She listens. She sees me. And that kiss…" My throat tightened. "I've been chasing that feeling for years. Never found it again."

Dre tilted his head. "So, what's the holdup?"

"Eddie," I said flatly. "He still lives in her head. I saw it the other night— she damn near folded when she saw that niggah walk in. I get it. She doesn't trust easily. But it feels like I'm fighting ghosts."

"Then fight 'em," Dre said simply. "Show her you're not that man. Hold her without clipping her wings."

His words echoed after he left. I turned back to my desk, pen in hand, but the truth pulsed like a verdict waiting to be read: I didn't just want another night. I wanted the mornings after, the weeks ahead, the years I hadn't even lived yet.

So, I grabbed my phone.

Antwon: *I need to ask you something. Friday night. Over dinner. Just us.*

Dana: *That sounds serious.*

Antwon: *It is. Not heavy. Just honest.*

Dana: *Okay. Dinner it is.*

Antwon: *Pack a bag. I don't want the night to end because of the clock.*

Dana: *…I'll be there.*

I leaned back in my chair, the glow of her name still on my screen.

Hayzel Greene

For years, I'd carried her memory like unfinished business.

Now?

It finally felt like a beginning.

Beyond the Dare

Chapter 10 – Dana

Friday night always carried its own weight—end of the week, start of possibility. I packed slowly, folded, and refolded clothes like the bag itself could expose me. He'd said dinner. Just dinner. But still… I slipped into a change of clothes, heels I hadn't worn in months, and lingerie so delicate it felt like a secret pressed against my skin. Not that I planned to wear it. But in case.

The drive over was short—too short. My nerves rattled like dice in a cup until the car turned into his neighborhood. Antwon's townhouse sat clean and modern, porch light spilling warm against the night. He stood in the doorway, casual in dark slacks and a crisp shirt, watching me approach like I was something worth waiting for.

"You really know how to shut a room down," he murmured as I stepped inside, eyes roaming but never disrespectful. The way his gaze slid over me sent a rush through me that I tried—and failed—to hide.

His home was tidy, masculine without being cold. A hint of his cologne lingered in the air, blending with the rich scent of steak.

"You cooked?" I teased.

He grinned. "Or at least took the credit for it."

Dinner was simple—steak, asparagus, garlic mashed potatoes—but thoughtful. We ate at his table, candles low, wine smooth. Conversation was easy at first—work, weekend plans, stories about my girls that had him laughing hard enough to put his fork down.

But when I asked about his week, about how he juggled cases, he leaned back, expression softening. "Honestly? The courtroom takes up a lot. But with you... it feels lighter. Like I can leave the fight outside."

I swallowed, suddenly unsure where to rest my eyes. "You say that now. But what happens when I stop feeling... light?"

His gaze held steady. "Then I'll hold steady. You don't have to be light all the time. I'm not here to erase Eddie or your past. I'm here because I want a future with you. Whatever pace that takes."

The words lodged in my chest. I wanted to believe him. Needed to believe him. And then he said the thing that broke me open:

"If tonight you want space, the guest room is yours. No pressure. Your call."

For a second, it almost made me laugh. After Vegas—after what we did, the way we burned through each other like fire on gasoline—him offering me a guest room felt almost absurd. The expectation should've been that tonight would be a repeat, another reckless night that left us tangled in sheets and memory.

But then he gave me that wry half-smile, like he'd read my thoughts.

"I know we've already... been there. Vegas was unforgettable. But this, us, now. I don't want it to be about expectation. I want it to be about choice."

The fact that he was offering a choice hit different. He wasn't trying to score points. He wasn't trying to cash in on the memory of what we'd already done. Offering me space wasn't weakness it was control. Courtesy. And somehow, that turned me on more than any guarantee of sex ever could.

Vegas had been wild, reckless heat. But this? This was restraint. Respect. Proof that he wanted more than just my body. Proof that he wanted me.

We moved to the couch with wine, the TV humming low but ignored. Somewhere between a sip and a laugh, my shoulder brushed his chest. I could feel his heat through the thin fabric of my dress.

The kiss started with me. Just a tilt of my head, a meeting of lips, soft but deliberate. He didn't lunge. Didn't push. Just let me set the pace until it deepened, until the wineglass trembled in my hand and I had to put it down.

By the time he lifted me into his arms, the question of the guest room was gone.

We went upstairs, the world narrowed to heat and heartbeat. Clothes slipped away between kisses—his shirt tugged over his head; my dress unzipped with trembling fingers.

He paused, eyes sweeping over me like I was art he'd been waiting years to see again. "Damn, Dana…" he whispered, reverent. "I tried. God knows I tried. But nothing, nobody… was ever like this."

I kissed him, urgently, and hungrily. Vegas had been wild, reckless. This was deeper. His hands moved slowly, then fast, mapping my skin, pulling sounds from my throat I didn't know I still had in me.

He pushed me back onto the bed, tugging my panties down—slow, deliberate, like he wanted me to beg. Cool air hit my skin, and then his mouth was on me.

His tongue dragged from the bottom of my slit all the way up, a wet, deliberate stroke that made my back arch. He circled my clit once, teasing, then sealed his lips around it, sucking hard until my thighs trembled. He shifted lower, tongue plunging inside me, stroking, curling, tasting me so deep I cried out his name. His hands clamped my thighs open as his tongue alternated—inside, then back to my clit—licking, flicking, sucking until I saw stars behind my eyelids.

I clawed at the sheets, moaning, every nerve alive. The pressure built, coiled tight, snapped. I shattered, screaming, my release flooding his tongue. He stayed there, licking me through it, long, slow strokes until my legs gave out beneath me. When he finally pulled back, his mouth glistened, his chin wet, his eyes pure hunger.

He crawled up my body, kissed me with my taste still on his lips, then pressed into me—thick, hard, stretching me so deep I gasped.

"Shit," he hissed, forehead pressed to mine. "You feel the same. Tighter, wetter—fuck."

Every thrust was deep, hard, relentless. The bed creaked, sheets twisted. My nails dug into his back, dragging lines that made him groan. He pinned my wrists above my head, hips slamming into mine, and I cried out with every stroke.

"You're mine," he growled into my ear. "Say it."

"I'm yours," I panted, chest heaving. "I'm yours, Antwon."

His rhythm turned savage, pounding me into the mattress. My body clenched around him, milking him, pulling him deeper. The heat built, hotter, sharper, until I shattered again, screaming, every nerve exploding.

He followed with a guttural roar, driving into me once, twice before spilling inside. His face pressed into my neck, his breath ragged, his body trembling against mine.

For a long moment, we stayed locked together, our skin slick, the sheets tangled. His heartbeat thundered against my chest, his arms holding me so tight I couldn't have moved if I wanted to.

"Vegas was unforgettable," he murmured into my hair. "But this... this feels like destiny."

I closed my eyes, chest heaving, and for the first time in years, I let the thought sit without fear.
Maybe he was right.

The room was quiet except for our uneven breaths, the thud of his heartbeat steady against my back. Slowly, the fire gave way to calmness I hadn't known I needed. His hand traced lazy circles on my hip, grounding me, tethering me in the best way.

"You, okay?" he whispered into my hair.

I smiled, small but real. "Better than okay."

He chuckled low, the sound vibrating against my skin. "Good. Because I was nervous as hell."

That made me laugh—soft, incredulous. "Nervous? After Vegas?"

"Yeah." He shifted to look at me, brushing damp curls from my cheek. "Vegas was wild. Amazing. But this?" His thumb lingered just beneath my lip. "This mattered. I didn't want to mess it up."

My throat tightened at the sincerity in his voice. I pressed a kiss to his chest, right over his heart. "You didn't."

We lay there like that, wrapped up in the warmth of us, until sleep began to pull us under. For the first time in years, I felt safe enough to drift, not knowing what morning would bring but certain he'd still be there.

Chapter 11 – Antwon

The morning light cut across my bedroom in pale stripes, but I'd been awake long before it touched me.

Dana was still asleep, her back warm against my chest, her breathing slow and steady. My arm draped over her waist like it had found its rightful place. For a long time, I didn't move. I just breathed her in—soft skin, faint trace of her perfume, the scent of last night still clinging to us both.

Vegas had been fire—reckless, wild—but this… this was something else. She hadn't just given me her body; she'd given me trust. Even if it was only a sliver, it was more valuable than anything I'd ever been handed. And God, it shook me.

The reel of last night played behind my eyes, sharper with every frame. The way she trembled under my mouth, the taste of her release spilling across my tongue, her cries breaking as I drove into her deeper, harder. Her nails raked down my back, claiming me as much as I claimed her. The moment her walls clenched tight around me, and she called my name—I could've died right then and felt complete.

I stirred just remembering it, pressing against her hip even as she slept. Every instinct said wake her, pull her on top of me, start again. But something steadier held me back—she deserved a morning without demands.

So, I stayed still, letting the quiet settle over us. Her cheek brushed my shoulder, the same shoulder that carried weight in courtrooms but had carried only her last night. My frame was built for fights and pressure, but lying here with Dana made me feel like my strength finally had purpose.

Still… God, I'd never been addicted to anything like this.

My mind flickered to Eddie the way Dana's shoulders folded when his name came up, the way her voice went small. I hated it. Hated that his shadow still lingered. She deserved to feel powerful. Desired. Safe.

I knew one night could not erase years of hurt, but last night our laughter over dinner, her hand gripping mine when she told me about him, the way she came apart under me later told me she wanted to try. And if she gave me the chance, I would prove every damn day that she was worth more than the scars he left behind.

My phone buzzed on the nightstand. I reached carefully so I would not wake her. A text from Dre lit up the screen:

Well? You locked in or what?

I smirked, shaking my head. Leave it to Dre to pick the worst possible moment. I typed back one-handed:

Not locked. But close. Real close.

Sliding the phone away, I looked at her again. Sunlight caught the curve of her shoulder, making her skin glow like poured honey. In her sleep, her fingers found mine, curling unconsciously.

Hayzel Greene

There were still pieces of her story I didn't know—like what had really led her to me that night in Vegas. But I knew one thing: I wasn't letting her walk back out.

I tightened my hold, lips brushing her hairline. This wasn't nostalgic. This wasn't me chasing a Vegas memory. This was the start of something real— if I didn't screw it up.

I made a quiet vow right there, as the sun climbed higher:
I'd be patient, but persistent. Gentle, but unshakable.
Whatever it took, Dana would know—Eddie was her past.
I intended to be her future.

Beyond the Dare

Chapter 12 – Dana

The morning light slipped through the curtains, gentle and forgiving. I blinked against it, stretched, and felt warmth beside me. Antwon's arm was heavy across my waist, his chest steady against my back.

For a moment, I didn't move. I just let myself feel.

It felt good. Too good.

His heat pressed into me; his breathing moved slowly and even against my shoulder. The echo of his hands on me last night still hummed through me like a low current. My thighs pressed together at the memory, a flush rising before I could stop it.

Vegas had been wild. Reckless. A dare. But last night, last night had been slow and scorching, deeper than anything I'd expected. I hadn't just surrendered my body; I'd let him in far enough to touch the places I usually kept locked.

And my body remembered. Moist heat pooled between my thighs just thinking about it, a reminder of how completely he'd undone me.

I rolled the thought over like a coin between my fingers. The sex had been fire, yes—but it was more than that. His patience. His choice to give me a choice. The way he'd said "guest room" even though we both knew how the night would end. It hadn't been about courtesy—it had been respect. That was the difference. That was what Vegas hadn't had.

I thought about Eddie, about the years I'd wasted trying to patch myself back together after he shredded me with betrayal. His shadow used to loom over me, whispering that I wasn't enough, that men always left. But last night he proved wrong.

When Eddie strutted into that restaurant, Antwon hadn't flinched. He hadn't folded. He'd squeezed my hand, stood firm at my side, and then, later, he'd made love to me like I was the only woman on earth. Like Eddie never existed.

And for the first time, I believed it. Eddie didn't own me anymore.

I turned slowly, facing Antwon. He was still asleep, lashes low, lips parted just enough to make me smile. He looked younger like that. Softer. Vulnerable, even.

Something inside me shifted.

The girls would never let me forget that one dare in Vegas had led me here. But what had started as a challenge, a game, had turned into something I never expected: a man who saw me, who wanted me beyond the surface, who made me feel whole again.

I wasn't there all the way yet. My guard wasn't completely down. But the wall was cracking, piece by piece, and I wasn't afraid of what might come through.

Last night was proof: Antwon wasn't chasing a memory. He was building something. And maybe—just maybe—I was ready to build with him.

Hayzel Greene

I brushed my fingers lightly across his chest, memorizing the heat and weight, before slipping quietly out of bed. My overnight bag sat waiting by the chair. I'd shower, dress, and head back to my world soon enough.

But for the first time in years, I wasn't thinking about what I'd lost.

I was thinking about what I'd just found.

Beyond the Dare

Chapter 13 – Antwon

The courtroom buzzed with tension, but I barely heard it. My eyes tracked the jury, every flicker of doubt cutting sharper than the last. I'd come in sharp this morning, suit pressed, arguments clean, confidence steady. But then my witness buckled. On cross, she froze—hesitated once, then contradicted herself. The opposing counsel tore into her like a wolf scenting blood, and by the time the judge called recess, the damage was done.

My client's eyes clung to me, wide and brittle, as if I'd dropped her from a height. The press scribbled like they knew the verdict. And for the first time in years, I did not see the path back.

The case adjourned until Monday. I walked out with my jaw tight, my gut sore. No theatrics. No swagger. Just the weight of failure pressing down with every step.

Back at the office, I ripped off my jacket and loosened my tie until it hung useless around my neck. I spread the files across my desk like a man dissecting his own mistakes. Timelines. Witness statements. Cross notes. The words blurred until they were nothing but ink smudges. My voice filled the empty room, muttering arguments that sounded hollow, dead-on arrival.

Still, no win. Not this time.

I dropped into my chair, head in my hands. Four years of victories. A reputation built on precision, on control. And here I was—unraveling.

My phone lit up beside me. I picked it up, thumb hovering. I typed one line. Deleted it. Typed another. Deleted again. Everything sounded like weakness.

Finally, I left the words bare. No explanation. No polish. Just raw truth. *Bad day. Don't think I can pull this one back.*

I hit send before I could stop myself.

Setting the phone face down, I leaned back in my chair, eyes closed. For once, I didn't want to be Antwon Carrington—the attorney, the steady hand, the man everyone counted on.

I just wanted to be a man, wondering if he still had it in him.

Chapter 14 – Dana

I read his message twice, maybe three times. *Bad day. Don't think I can pull this one back.*

Antwon wasn't the kind of man to wave a white flag. For him to sound defeated? That was bigger than the words on the screen.

I sat on the edge of my bed, staring at the phone, then at my overnight bag leaning against the dresser. Thirty minutes. That's what it would take me to get to him. Thirty minutes of highway and second-guessing myself.

Am I intruding? Will he think I'm pushing too hard?

But then I pictured him alone, stewing in silence, drowning in pressure. And I knew.

I pulled the bag close and started packing: A pair of slacks and a blouse for work on Monday, just in case, flats for comfort, and, almost without thinking, my favorite silk nightgown. Something about the careful fold of fabric into the bag made my pulse quicken. This wasn't just a visit. This was me choosing him.

The drive was heavy with doubt, but determination carried me through. By the time I pulled into his building, my nerves had hardened into resolve.

He opened the door on the second knock. The sight of him gutted me—tie loose, sleeves rolled, dark circles under his eyes. Papers scattered across the table like a storm had blown through.

"You didn't have to come," he said, voice rough, half a protest.

"I know." I stepped inside anyway, holding up the takeout bag. "But I wanted to."

For a moment, we just looked at each other. Something shifted in his expression—relief, maybe, or something he didn't want to name.

He paced while I set the food down, he started talking about witnesses and timelines, evidence that didn't hold up. I let him vent. Then I asked questions, the kind I'd ask at work—about gaps, order of operations, what slipped through the cracks. Slowly, the frantic edge in his voice softened. He sat, spread the files out again, and listened while I pointed at details he'd overlooked.

"Wait." He pulled one document closer, eyes narrowing. "That… that changes everything. If I connect this, it shifts the whole timeline."

For the first time that night, his eyes lit. Not cocky, not smug—just sharp again. Hopeful.

"Dana…" His voice was steadier now. "You just gave me something I didn't see."

I shrugged, warmth blooming in my chest. "Project managers are professional puzzle solvers. Just happened to be yours tonight."

He exhaled, shoulders loosening. The weight of defeat seemed to slip, just a little.

"Enough about court," I said gently, brushing his arm. "You need to breathe."

He chuckled, tired but real. "You always know how to check me, don't you?"

I smiled, meaning only to comfort, but the moment my hand lingered against him, the air shifted. His fingers curled around mine, slow, deliberate. He stopped pacing. He looked at me like I was the one thing tethering him to the ground.

The kiss started tentative, a question. When I leaned in to answer it, his lips pressed harder, and heat roared to life. His frustration melted into me, his sigh vibrating against my mouth.

I pressed closer, molding against his chest. His hand slid to the back of my neck, deepening the kiss until it wasn't soft anymore—it was hunger, it was fire. Teeth grazed, tongues tangled, and he groaned rough and low.

By the time we reached the bedroom, his jacket was already on the floor, my blouse hanging open, my bra strap sliding uselessly off my shoulder. His hands were everywhere—cupping, tugging, gripping like he couldn't decide what part of me to claim first.

He lay me back, hovering above me, chest heaving. Then his mouth trailed down my throat, biting lightly at my shoulder before moving lower. My blouse fell away, my bra undone, and his tongue circled my nipple—slow at first, then greedy. I gasped, arching into him, my fingers knotted in his hair.

"God, Dana…" he growled against my skin. "You feel better than I remembered."

He kissed lower, down my stomach, tongue tracing my hip before dragging between my thighs. My skirt was gone, panties tugged aside, and then his mouth was on me.

The first lick was deliberate from the bottom to top, slow enough to make my back arch. He circled my clit with the tip of his tongue, teasing, then sealed his lips around it, sucking hard until I cried out.

"Antwon!"

He groaned into me, the vibration sending shockwaves through my body. His tongue slid inside me, curling deep while his fingers joined in, pumping until my thighs shook and my moans filled the room. The orgasm ripped through me violently and sharply, my scream breaking against his name.

When he finally pulled up, his chin glistened with me. He kissed me, messy, hungry, like he wanted me to taste myself on his tongue.

And then he pushed inside.

The stretch stole my breath—thick, deep, filling me so completely my nails dug into his back. He cursed, forehead pressed to mine. "Fuck. You're perfect. I need this... I need _you_."

Every thrust was harder, deeper, shaking the bed. My heels dug into his back, my legs locked around his waist, dragging him closer.

"I've got you," he whispered, desperate now. "Don't leave me in this alone."

"I won't," I gasped, clutching him tight. "I'm here, Antwon."

His hips drove faster, his body slamming into mine. I screamed as another orgasm tore through me, clenching around him so tight he roared, burying himself deep, spilling hot inside me as his body shook.

He collapsed against me, chest heaving, lips pressed to my neck. His arm wrapped around me, holding me like he needed proof I was real.

And for the first time that day, he finally let go.

I closed my eyes, sinking into him, the words clear in my mind:

This wasn't just sex. It was a surrender. His need tangled with mine, proof that the flame between us hadn't burned out—it had only been waiting for air.

This was what it meant to show up.

Beyond the Dare

Chapter 15 – Antwon

I woke before dawn; the city still wrapped in quiet. The room was dim, with only the faint glow of the streetlights slipping through the blinds. Dana was asleep beside me, hair sprawled across the pillow, one hand resting lightly on my chest.

For a long time, I didn't move. I just let myself breathe her in, memorizing the weight of her against me. Not Vegas, not a memory—here. Real. And it wasn't just last night's fire that lingered. It was the calm after. The way her body relaxed into mine like she trusted me to hold it. That reminder alone made the weight of today's trial feel lighter.

Still, routine tugged at me. Court days didn't wait.

I slipped out of bed, padded into the kitchen, and moved through my muscle memory, eggs, toast, coffee. Nothing fancy, just the same steady breakfast that grounded me before every appearance. But this time, I made enough for two.

When it was ready, I set a plate on the table and carried a mug back to the bedroom. She stirred when I brushed her shoulder, eyes blinking open slowly, sleepy, beautiful.

"Morning," I said softly.

"It's still dark out," she murmured, voice husky from sleep.

"Court waits for no one." I smiled faintly. "Breakfast is on the table. Eat before you head out."

She shifted, pulling the sheet higher, and the sight of her there—hair tousled, skin still flushed from the night before—made me want to forget the courtroom altogether. I leaned down, kissed her forehead, then her lips—slow, lingering, reluctant to pull away.

"Lock up when you leave," I whispered.

Her fingers caught my wrist, light but deliberate. She held me there for a breath longer than necessary, her lips parting like she wanted to say something. I waited, but no words came, just a quiet nod, her eyes searching mine.

"Go win your case," she finally said.

That pulled a real smile out of me. "That's the plan."

I slipped free, grabbed my briefcase, jacket over my arm, and stepped out into the still-sleeping city. The weight of the day pressed down as it always did—but this time, it pressed softer. Because for the first time in years, I wasn't walking into the fight alone.

Chapter 16 – Dana

The door shut behind him, and silence filled the townhouse. I sat at the kitchen table, staring at the plate he'd left me, steam still curling from the eggs and coffee. It felt strangely intimate—him feeding me before walking into battle.

I ate slowly, replaying last night in my head. His frustration, my decision to come, the way he'd looked at me after we pieced together a new angle for his case. The way he'd kissed me like I was more than comfort, more than distraction.

When the food was gone, I set my fork down but didn't move. Work waited thirty minutes away—spreadsheets, deadlines, endless meetings. But my heart wasn't there.

I pictured him standing in court alone, shoulders heavy with a case that had already drained him. The image twisted something deep inside me.

And then Eddie's ghost tried to creep in. I could almost hear him, scoffing the way he always did whenever I showed up for him: *"Why are you here? Nobody needs to see you. Don't make this about you."* Eddie never wanted me to be visible. He liked his secrets too much, his double life tucked neat behind closed doors. Support, to him, was silent. Invisible. Convenient.

Antwon wasn't Eddie. He wasn't afraid of being seen with me. He wanted me there. He'd shown me that repeatedly.

Still, doubt whispered as I glanced at the clock. *Will he think I'm pushing too hard? Crowding him?*

But underneath the nerves were something steadier, stronger: certainty.

If he could fight for me, stand firm against my shadows, then I could damn sure show up for him when the weight threatened to break him.

I cleaned the dishes, straightened the counter, and grabbed my bag. As I locked the door behind me, I whispered into the quiet townhouse, almost like he could hear me:

"You're not doing this alone."

Then I slid into my car, pointed it toward the courthouse, and hit the gas.

Chapter 17 – Antwon

The courthouse had its own kind of hum. Not the buzzing chaos of an airport or the steady chatter of a restaurant—but a low, nervous energy, like the air itself held its breath.

Dana slipped into the gallery just as the bailiff called the court to order. Her heels clicked softly against the tile before she sank into a wooden bench. The room was crowded with clients, reporters, a sketch artist who took his place in the far corner, already hunched over, pencil scratching, capturing every gesture as though it might matter later.

I didn't see her at first. My mind locked on the case; on the puzzle I'd nearly lost control of. But when I finally scanned the gallery and caught her eyes—steady, certain—I felt something click into place inside me.
She came.

The judge banged his gavel, pulling me back. "Mr. Carrington, you may proceed."

I stood, straightened my jacket, and motioned to the clerk. "Your Honor, I'd like to recall Ms. Hensley to the stand."

A ripple of surprise moved through the room. The opposing counsel shot me a look—half annoyance, half disbelief. But the judge allowed it.

Ms. Hensley took the oath again, nervous as ever, but this time I had my angle. Dana's late-night questions had peeled back a layer I'd overlooked, and now I was ready to press.

"Ms. Hensley," I began, voice calm but firm, "yesterday you testified that the ledger entries from March 14th were made at 2 p.m., correct?"

She nodded. "Yes, that's what I said."

I picked up a document, stepped closer. "And yet, this timestamp" I pointed "shows 5:42 p.m. Can you explain that discrepancy?"

The gallery leaned forward.

Her eyes darted. "I, I must have been mistaken."

"Mistaken, or pressured?" I pressed, my tone steady but sharp.

Opposing counsel shot up. "Objection—argumentative."

The judge overruled. "The witness may answer."

Ms. Hensley's voice cracked. "I was told to say 2 p.m. by my supervisor. But it wasn't true. The entry was after hours."

Murmurs erupted. I let the weight of her words hang before turning back to the jury. "So, the defense's entire timeline—hinging on a midday entry—is false."

As I returned to my table, I didn't just see a win taking shape—I saw Dana's fingerprints on it.

~~~~~

Hayzel Greene
Closing Arguments

Opposing counsel blustered, waving hands, trying to paint me as overreaching. But the jury wasn't buying it. Their eyes slid back to me, waiting.

I rose for my turn, buttoning my jacket, walking slowly and deliberately.

"Ladies and gentlemen, you've heard the defense tell you one story. A story that crumbled the second light was shed on it. You saw it today—with your own eyes. A witness was pressured. A timeline bent. Evidence manipulated.

But facts don't lie. Timestamps don't change. And justice doesn't bow to intimidation."

I paused, letting my voice drop, my gaze swept across the box.

"You have a choice. Believe the smoke and mirrors—or trust what the evidence shows you. I know you'll make the right one."

~~~~~

The Verdict

The judge gave his instructions, sending the jury out. The room broke into restless chatter, tension thick. Dana sat still, hands folded in her lap, eyes on me. I could feel her faith across the room like a lifeline.

Minutes crawled into an hour. My chest tightened. Doubt crept in, sharp and suffocating, until the bailiff's voice boomed: "All rise."

The jury filed back in, faces unreadable. My pulse slammed in my ears.

The foreperson stood. "We, the jury, find the defendant… guilty."

For a moment, the courtroom froze in stunned silence. Then the eruption—clients crying, reporters scrambling, pens flying. The judge slammed his gavel.

"Order! ORDER!"

The gallery hushed, but the verdict still hung heavy, undeniably.

We'd won.

~~~~~

Aftermath

Outside, the courthouse steps swarmed with cameras and microphones. Flashbulbs popped, reporters shouted over each other, voices blending into chaos.

"Mr. Carrington, was the witness's second testimony a surprise?"
"Mr. Carrington, how did you turn the case around?"
"Mr. Carrington—Antwon—over here!"

I answered what I could, crisp and professional, but my eyes kept flicking to the edge of the crowd. Dana stood there, just far enough to stay out of the frenzy, watching.

Our gazes locked. The noise around me faded.

This was the story the press wanted. But she was the story I needed.

I excused myself from the cluster of microphones, stepped down, and crossed toward her. Cameras followed, but I didn't care.

Hayzel Greene

I reached for her hand, squeezed it tight.

"Couldn't have done this without you," I murmured, just for her.

Her smile bloomed, soft and certain. And in that moment, with the press shouting, the city buzzing, and the case behind me, I felt the real victory wasn't the verdict at all.

It was her.

Beyond the Dare

Chapter 18 – Dana

The verdict had been barely a week ago, but the air already felt lighter. Antwon had stood tall in that courtroom, turned the case around, and walked out a winner. But when the cameras cleared and the weight was off his shoulders, he surprised me.

"Let's get away," he said that night, voice low but certain. "Not just us—bring your girls. I'll bring Dre. Family. Fun. We all could use it."

It caught me off guard. Most men wanted me all to themselves or at least pretended to. But Antwon knew better. He knew Danielle, Sam, and Lani weren't just friends, they were family. He didn't compete with that. He welcomed it.

So, when I started packing, it wasn't just swimsuits and sandals. It was joy. It was a possibility. It was a version of myself I hadn't touched in too long—lighter, softer, unbothered.

~~~~~

Port Day

Salt and sunscreen clung to the air as the ship rose out of the water like a floating city. Its horn vibrated straight through my chest.

Danielle and Sam spotted me in the terminal, waving like rescue flags.

"Vacation face!" Sam shouted, arms wide.

Danielle spun me before I could hug her. "Turn around, let me see the dress. Okay, I approve."

Lani appeared with sleek sunglasses and a grin she tried to hide. "Ladies."

And then Antwon. Dimples flashing, calm like he owned the crowd. He kissed my cheek like we were already alone.

"Ready?"

"Since Tuesday," I said, and meant it.

We boarded with the slow tide of people—perfumes, chatter, kids tugging parents along. The atrium opened above us, chandeliers catching light, the steel drum music bouncing off the walls. Crew members pressed champagne flutes into our hands, something citrusy and cold that tasted like permission.

"Dre!" Antwon called, and his cousin strode up—grinning, gold hoop glinting.

"So, this is the famous Dana?" Dre asked, already shaking his head like restraint didn't exist. He pressed a hand to his chest, crooning, "I'm spruuung…"

Danielle snorted. "Not T-Pain."

"Oh, I got range," Dre said, pivoting to her. "Don't tempt me to do the bridge."

"You don't even know if this ship has a bridge," she shot back.

He laughed, delighted. "Oh, you are dangerous. You must be Danielle."

"That's me."

"Then I'm in trouble."

We all laughed, the kind of easy warmth that made the ship feel less like a floating city and more like our own world.

~~~~~

Sail Away

We will hit the cabins first, then the pool, followed by the deck. The ocean started to swallow the land as it slid back from the ship. The DJ had aunties and kids in the same dance line, Sam negotiating drink refills like she ran the bar, Lani capturing everything like a producer, Danielle and Dre volleying between flirt and banter.

Antwon slid behind me, one hand at my waist, thumb brushing slow circles. His breath was warm in my ear.

"Good idea?" he murmured.

"The best," I whispered.

~~~~~

Dinner

The dining hall was pristine. There were white tablecloths everywhere, low chatter from guests and the slight roar of the ship as it carried us to sea. We grouped up in a corner and sat for dinner. Sam working on the bread baskets, Lani critiquing appetizers, Danielle, and Dre playing verbal chess.

Antwon leaned close. "I like your people."

"They're a lot," I warned, smiling.

"Good," he said simply. "You deserve a lot."

~~~~~

Night

After dessert, the ship glowed like a dream—casino clatter, piano crooning, couples strolling the plush hallways. Antwon and I peeled away from the group with just a look.

Up on the upper deck, stars stretched endlessly across a velvet black sky. The breeze tangled my hair until he smoothed it back, his fingers lingering on my neck. My knees weakened under his touch.

"Here?" I breathed, half-shocked, half-desperate.
"Here," he said, rough, certain.

Hayzel Greene

The rest of the night belonged to him—the ocean roaring below, my cries carried by the wind, his mouth claiming me until I shook, until I begged, until nothing else existed but us.

When he finally pushed inside, filling me deep, my body breaking open around him, the truth hit me harder than the waves slamming the ship's hull:

Vegas was a dare.
This felt like ours.

Beyond the Dare

Chapter 19 – Antwon

The night on the ship felt alive and the lights glittering like a city, casino bells chiming, piano music drifting up from somewhere below. None of it mattered. The only thing I saw was Dana.

One look was all it took. No words, no excuses. Just us breaking from the group, her steps syncing with mine until we reached the upper deck, where the air bit cooler and the stars hung so close it felt like they belonged to us.

The ocean stretched black and endless. Her hair whipped wild in the wind, and I smoothed it back with one hand, my thumb tracing the hollow of her throat.

"Good idea?" I asked, my voice low, already thick with what I wanted. "The best," she whispered.

That was all I needed.

The kiss started slowing—testing, savoring—but she melted into me, lips parting like she'd been waiting. Hunger roared to life. My hand slid beneath her dress, fingertips grazing her thigh. Her breath hitched, and her eyes went wide.

"Here?" she whispered, half-shocked, half-desperate. "Here," I told her, no hesitation.

The ship rocked beneath us, the ocean roaring below, and I dropped to my knees. I shoved her dress higher, panties aside, spreading her open.

"Fuck," I groaned the second I tasted her. "I missed this."

I dragged my tongue from the bottom to top, slowly, savoring the slick heat of her. Her moan tore off into the wind, straight through me. She was shaking already, clutching the rail, stars blurring above her head as I sucked her clit into my mouth and flicked my tongue fast until she was gasping, grinding into me.

"Taste so good, baby," I muttered against her. "You want to come on my tongue?"
"Yes—please—don't stop—"

That begging undid me. I slid two fingers inside her, curling, pumping, relentless while my mouth worked her clit. Her thighs trembled around my head, her cries shredded by the wind.
"Come on, Dana," I urged, sucking harder. "Let go for me."

She broke, screaming my name, her release flooding hot across my tongue. I licked her through it, swallowed it down like I'd been starving for her.

When I stood, chin wet, mouth glistening, I kissed her hard, messy, making sure she tasted herself on me. "Now I need to feel you," I growled, yanking at my zipper.

Hayzel Greene

I spun her, bent her against the rail, and shoved inside one deep stroke.
The heat of her wrapped me so tight I had to bite back a roar.
"Fuck—you're so damn tight. Like this pussy was made for me."

Every thrust slammed her against the railing, the sway of the ship syncing
with my rhythm. I gripped her hips hard, pulling her back into me,
pounding until the sound of skin on skin rivaled the ocean's roar.

"Say it's mine," I rasped in her ear, teeth scraping her neck.
"It's yours," she gasped, voice breaking. "All yours, Antwon!"

Her body clamped down on me, milking me, dragging me closer to the
edge. I reached around, thumb grinding her clit until she screamed again,
spasming around me.
"Shit—fuck, I feel you coming all over me," I groaned, pounding faster,
my body seizing. "You're gonna make me—fuck—"

The heat snapped, and I roared, burying deep, spilling inside her, shaking
as she clenched tight around me. My chest collapsed against her back,
breath ragged, sweat dripping onto her skin.

But I couldn't stop. Not with her. Not tonight.

We stumbled inside, leaving the balcony door wide open so the salt air
poured in. I lay her back on the bed, spread her thighs, and buried my
mouth between them again. She whimpered, raw, but I licked her slowly,
savoring, my tongue plunging deep until she writhed.

"Please, Antwon" she begged, breathless.

"You think I'm finished?" I said against her, voice low. "Nah, baby. Not until you can't remember your own name."

She shattered again on my tongue, and only when she went limp did, I climb over her, sliding back inside, slower this time. Grinding deep. Making love to her as much as fucking her.

Her arms locked around me, nails clawing my back, her lips desperate on my throat.

"I'm here," I whispered between thrusts. "I'm not going anywhere."

We came together again, slower, deeper, like vows etched into skin.

After, she curled into me, the ocean breeze cooling our sweat, the ship rocking steadily beneath us. I held her close, staring out at the horizon, certain of what I already knew.

Vegas had been a dare.

This was destiny.

Chapter 20 – Dana

Home always hits differently after being away. The rhythm of the city, the hum of traffic, the same corner store with the same clerk who barely looked up like nothing had changed. And yet, everything had.

Dragging my suitcase through the front door, I paused in the quiet. The apartment felt too still after days of laughter, ocean breezes, and stolen kisses under the stars. I'd left part of myself out there on that ship—with him.

The cruise had been… more than a trip. More than cocktails with my girls or late-night jokes from Dre that had Danielle blushing. It had been proven that Antwon wasn't just talking. He showed up every moment. For me. With me. And now that we were back on land, I couldn't pretend I didn't want more.

I unpacked slowly, folding clothes that still carried the faint salt of the sea. A napkin from one of the dinners slipped out of my bag, faint traces of his cologne clinging to it. My chest tightened. His hand warm at my back, his voice steady when he said he wanted not just trips, but the regular days. The ordinary with me.

Ordinary. I'd spent years chasing extraordinarily to numb the ache Eddie left behind. Coming home from him always meant emptiness, silence, loneliness that wrapped tightly. But this was different. With Antwon, ordinary felt like something I could trust—something that could still be extraordinary.

My phone buzzed. A message from the group chat. Danielle: Made it home! Already missing y'all.

Sam: Back to reality. Somebody hurry up and send me a cocktail, please.

Lani: Best trip ever. My cheeks still hurt from laughing.

I smiled, typing my own check-in. Then another notification slid across my screen.

Antwon: Are you home safe?

Three little words, but they rooted deep. He could've just assumed. Could've waited. But he wanted to know. He wanted to be sure.

Me: Yes. Just walked in.

…Already feels too quiet without you.

The dots blinked, then his reply came:

Antwon: Good. Rest. Let me know when you're ready for dinner again. I want to see you before the week gets away from us.

I set the phone down, smiling in silence. For once, coming home didn't feel like the end of something. It felt like the beginning.

The suitcase could wait. Tomorrow I can wait. Tonight, I let myself believe.

Chapter 21 – Antwon

Sunday night, I took Dana to dinner. Not the kind of dinner where cameras flashed or where every course had a name you couldn't pronounce. Just a quiet table for two, tucked in the corner of a bistro with soft jazz and low lights.

She wore a simple dress, nothing flashy, but on her it looked better than runway. She laughed over a glass of wine, telling me a story about Sam arguing with a bartender on the ship, and I swore the whole restaurant dimmed around her.

For the first time in weeks, I wasn't thinking about cases or deadlines. Just her.

"You're quiet," she said, tilting her head, reading me like she always did.

"Just taking this in," I admitted. "Us. Here. Feels good."

Her smile softened. "Good. Because you deserve a break from always carrying the weight of the world on your shoulders."

I wanted to tell her then—that sometimes the weight doesn't come from the courtroom, but from ghosts. That I felt one circling us, waiting. But I bit it back. No sense in souring the night without reason.

Instead, I reached across the table, threading my fingers through hers. "Whatever this week brings, I want you to know something."

Her eyes lifted, curious.

"I'm in this. Not just for weekends, or trips, or wins in the courtroom. I'm in it for the quiet moments too. For all of it."

Her thumb brushed my knuckle, a smile ghosting across her lips. "Me too."

That vow sat between us for the rest of the night—unspoken, but real. By the time I walked her to her door, kissed her slowly and deep, I thought maybe I could outrun the shadows for good.

But Monday proved me wrong.

~~~~~

Monday mornings always smelled like burnt coffee and overworked air conditioning at the firm. By eight, I was already at my desk, flipping through briefs, mentally preparing for the week's hearings. The cruise glow had faded, but Dana lingered in my veins like a steady hum.

That hum cut out the second Marcus, one of the senior partners, knocked on my open door.

"Carrington, got a new client for you," he said, dropping a thick folder on my desk. "High-profile. Paid the retainer up front. Asked for you specifically."

That wasn't unusual—my last few wins had me in demand. But when I opened the file, the name staring back at me froze the air in my lungs.

Eddie Thompson.

Hayzel Greene

For a long second, all I could do was stare. The same Eddie Dana had told me about in quiet, trembling tones. The man who had shredded her trust like it was paper.

I forced my jaw to unclench. "Why me?" I asked, keeping my voice level.

Marcus shrugged. "Said he remembered you introduced yourself as an attorney once, and then he saw you on TV after the Stokes case. Impressed. Said he wanted the best." He smirked. "Who are we to argue? The man cut a check that makes saying no impossible."

I nodded tightly, but inside, every muscle was wound like a spring. Eddie. Of all people.

When the conference room door opened later that afternoon, my gut confirmed what the folder had warned. Eddie strolled in like he owned the place, a smug curve on his lips, and extended his hand.

"Antwon Carrington," I said before he could speak, my voice crisp, controlled. "Attorney, Carrington & Associates."

His grip was firm, his eyes just as sharp as I remembered them from that restaurant—when he'd looked back at Dana like he still had some kind of claim.

"Glad you're taking my case," Eddie said, sliding into a chair. "I told the partners I wanted you, specifically. You got a way of handling yourself."

I didn't smile. Didn't blink. I sat across from him, keeping my tone all business. "Let's get to it then. What exactly are we fighting for?"

But inside, my mind wasn't on the case. It was on Dana. On her voice the night before, promising to me she was in this. On her smile across that dinner table.

And in truth, I couldn't escape:

If I kept this from her and she found out later, it could undo everything we'd just built.

One thing was certain, Eddie might have walked into my office, but I wasn't going to let him walk back into Dana's life.

Not without going through me first.

Chapter 22 – Antwon

The office was quiet. Too quiet. Just the faint hum of the copier someone had forgotten to shut off and the muffled buzz of Akron nightlife bleeding through the windows. Normally, late nights didn't bother me—I'd pulled a lot of all-nighters prepping for trial—but tonight the silence pressed differently. Tight. Heavy.

The file sat open on my desk, thick with depositions and motions. Eddie Thompson. His name stamped across the front like it had every right to sit there.

Of all people.

Of all firms in Ohio.

Why mine?

I rubbed at my temples, staring at the retainer receipt. Substantial. Enough that the partners wouldn't even entertain me tossing it back. He hadn't just asked for "a lawyer." He'd asked for me. By name.

The bourbon on my desk had gone warm, but I lifted it anyway, the burn down my throat matching the boil under my collar. The memory played again, uninvited: Eddie swaggering into that restaurant with a woman on his arm, glancing back at Dana like she was still his to claim. That same smirk had been waiting for me in the conference room today.

"You introduced yourself as Attorney Carrington," he'd said, lounging in the chair like he owned the place. "Then I saw you on TV after that verdict. Figured, why not hire the best?"

Should've been flattering. But all I felt was the sour taste of fate's bad joke.

I leaned back in my chair, staring at the ceiling while the city's neon blinked faintly through the glass. How the hell was I supposed to tell Dana? She'd fought to bury him. And now, here he was—dragged back into her life through me.

If I told her straight, would she hear the truth—that this was business, forced, unavoidable? Or would she see betrayal? Would she think I'd opened the door to the very man she'd spent years locking out?

The worst part: I couldn't walk away. Not without consequences. The firm had cashed his check. To step off the case now would be malpractice, not just bad optics. Eddie knew that. Hell, maybe that was the point.

I set the glass down hard, the sound cracking against the silence. My mind spun back to the cruise—the kiss under the stars, Dana's laughter mixing with the ocean wind, her voice soft when she finally admitted she was willing to try again. She'd started letting me in, brick by brick. And this— Eddie—was the last shadow I wanted creeping back in to dim that light.

I clenched my fists, my jaw tight. "Not this time," I muttered into the empty office. "He's not winning twice."

But the truth lingered, heavier than the file in front of me:

Hayzel Greene

I'd promised Dana I wasn't going anywhere. But tonight, staring at Eddie's name across my desk, I wondered if fate was already testing how much that promise was worth.

Beyond the Dare

Chapter 23 – Dana

It had been two weeks since the cruise, but the ease we'd found at sea was already slipping on land. The laughter, the late-night balcony talks, the sense that nothing could touch us all felt farther away every time Antwon's eyes drifted somewhere I couldn't follow.

At first, I told myself it was just the case. Being with a lawyer meant long hours, late nights, and his phone buzzing with emails at all hours. I could live with that. What I couldn't shake was the way his mind seemed to drift when he was sitting right in front of me.

We were together more now—weekends, sometimes whole weeks if I worked remotely from Akron. His townhouse had started to feel like a second home. My toothbrush lived in his bathroom; my sweaters claimed a corner of his closet. By all accounts, we were a couple.

But sometimes I'd look across the table at him, mid-conversation, and realize he hadn't heard a word I'd said. His eyes glazed, fixed somewhere else, like he was replaying an argument in his head.

"Antwon?" I'd nudge, smiling to soften the edge.

He'd blink, refocus. "Sorry, baby. Just tired."

I wanted to believe that. But tired didn't explain the way his jaw clenched when he thought I wasn't looking, or how he'd sip slowly from his glass, buying time before changing the subject.

Nights were the hardest. Lying beside him, his arm heavy across my waist, his breathing steady—but every so often I'd feel him stir, shifting like sleep wouldn't hold. Once or twice, I'd opened my eyes and caught him staring at the ceiling, expression locked tight in thought.

"What's on your mind?" I whispered once.

"Nothing that matters," he murmured, kissing the top of my head. But his voice didn't match the words.

It wasn't distance I could measure in miles—it was measured in silence, in the weight between words.

I told myself to trust him, to let him carry whatever burden he was wrestling with until he was ready to share it. But deep down, something gnawed at me:
Whatever it was, it wasn't just work.

~~~~~

The morning marched like any other: coffee, two slices of toast, his quick eggs, soft music from the tiny speaker on the counter. He kissed my forehead first, then my mouth, lingering like he wanted normal to stick.

"Big day?" I asked, handing him his travel mug.

"Just… stacked," he said. The pause before the word stacked was thin as paper. "I'll text you."

He kissed me again at the door—once, twice, like punctuation—then was gone, cologne softening in the air behind him.

Hayzel Greene

Fine. Work would fill the quiet. I stripped the bed, opened the blinds, straightened his neat chaos into something less sprawl, telling myself I wasn't snooping. That's when I saw it—just a corner of a manila folder peeking from beneath a stack of color-coded binders.

Big block letters bled along the tab like a bruise.

THOMPSON, E.

My breath caught. My body knew it before my mind could reason it away.

I froze, hand hovering over the papers, like pausing before touching a hot pan even if the stove was off.

It could be any Thompson, E is a common initial.

You are in a law office, not a diary.

But memory had its own voice. And it whispered: You know who it is.

I straightened the stack, trying to tuck the name back under the pile, but my hand disobeyed. I slid the folder free, slow, feeling the weight of it.

"This is privileged," I whispered to the empty townhouse, as if saying it aloud might stop me. "It's not mine."

And yet, another truth pressed against my ribs: You've been sleeping next to a man who tastes like secrets.

I carried the folder to the bed like it might shatter if I moved too fast. Sat cross-legged, anchored me, and held the edge a second longer. Then I opened it.

~~~~~

The first page was clean fields and tidy boxes. Client: **Eddie Thompson.**

The name knocked the air from my lungs. My mind went straight back—the key in his door, the sound of laughter from the wrong room, his look that said *you're the one out of place.* Years of silence about it, and now here it was in print.

I read on because stopping would have been worse. Depo summaries. Email printouts. Timelines flagged with sticky notes. Every line confirmed it—Eddie's chaos wasn't just a memory anymore. It was documented. Catalogued.

Fear came first. Then anger. And beneath both, something I hadn't expected: relief. Because for once, his betrayal was more than just mine to carry. It was on paper now, undeniable.

Still—Antwon.

Antwon, who kissed me goodnight. Antwon, whose eyes had been distant all month. Antwon, who hadn't told me.

~~~~~

The door clicked. Keys rattled in the bowl.

"Dana?" His voice carried down the hall, warm, familiar. "You here, baby?"

I froze. The bed was scattered with paper; my notes were bright against the case file like bruises. My pulse roared in my ears.

Hayzel Greene

He stepped into the doorway. Stopped cold.

The distance he had been carrying all month slid off his face, replaced by something raw.

I looked up at him, a page trembling between my fingers.

My voice was steady, even though everything inside me cracked:

"You weren't going to tell me, were you?"

Beyond the Dare

Chapter 24 – Antwon

I knew something was off the second I stepped inside. The house was quiet—too quiet. No music playing, no clatter in the kitchen, no hum of her voice on a call.

"Dana?" I called out, loosening my tie as I kicked off my shoes.

No answer.

I moved down the hall toward the bedroom, and that is when I saw her.

She was cross-legged on the bed; papers scattered everywhere like fallen leaves. My papers. Eddie's file. Her eyes darted over the lines, sticky notes already marking sections, her expression a storm I could not read.

My chest dropped.

"Dana." My voice was sharper than I meant it to be.

She looked up, startled, guilt flashing in her eyes before stubbornness took over. "You left it here." Her voice was calm, but her hands gripped the papers tightly. "I didn't mean to, but once I saw his name—Antwon, I had to know."

Heat rose in me—frustration, fear, panic. "That's confidential." I stepped closer, jaw tight. "Do you realize what you are doing? That is evidence, testimony, private statements—"

"I know exactly what it is!" she snapped, cutting me off. Her chest rose and fell fast. "And you were not going to tell me. You have been… somewhere else for weeks now. Blank stares, half conversations. You sit right next to me, and I can feel you are a million miles away. This—" she waved at the file, "—this is why, isn't it?"

I ran a hand down my face, torn between anger and defeat. "Dana, I was not hiding it to hurt you. I did not know how to bring it up. Eddie retained the firm. He asked for me specifically. And once that retainer cleared, I could not just push it off my desk. It is not that simple."

Her laugh was bitter, sharp. "Not that simple? He is the man who broke me. Who made me doubt every piece of myself. And now he is back, sitting across from you like it's some game of fate. How do I not feel like I'm losing all over again?"

The fight drained out of me at her words. I crossed the room and sank onto the edge of the bed, close but not too close. "Dana, look at me. You're not losing. Not this time. He doesn't get to win twice."

Her eyes shimmered, but she blinked hard, pushing it down. Then something shifted in her. She straightened, gathered a few pages, and her tone cooled—businesslike.

"Alright, Attorney Carrington," she said, her project manager voice sliding into place. "You want to talk about it? Let's talk about it."

She shuffled the papers into order with quick, practiced hands, sticky notes already dividing sections. "I've been combing through this for hours. The timelines are messy. Your witness statements contradict three places. And this—" she tapped her finger on one page, where a line stood out in bold, *SUBJECT X – female associate, March 4, recurring presence*— "this is more than a coincidence. That's my birthday, Antwon. These descriptions? They sound like me."

My gut clenched.

"And it's not just me," Dana pushed, her voice hardening. "There are other women sprinkled through the notes—ghosts of his patterns. But *Subject X* shows up again. Wire transfers. Shell corporations. Meetings marked 'private.'" She shoved the page toward me. "Do you know what that means?"

I swallowed, my voice low. "It means Eddie was hiding money."

"It means Eddie was using me," she corrected. Her eyes locked on mine, fierce and wet. "You think I didn't recognize the breadcrumb? Years ago, he gave me a gift—a little black lockbox, said it was for keepsakes. I shoved it in a closet. I never thought twice. But now? Now I wonder if that wasn't a keepsake at all. If it were the key to one of these accounts."

Her words hit me like a fist.

"Dana…" I started, but she didn't let me finish.

"Do you see it now?" she demanded. "This isn't just any case file. Eddie hired you because of me. Because he knows I would never sit in a room with him, never listen to a word he said. But if the man I'm with is on the other side of the table, maybe he thinks he'll get close enough. That through you, he'll find a way back to me—and to that money."

Silence stretched between us, thick as the papers scattered around us. My pulse thudded in my ears. And for the first time in years, the man who always had the answers… didn't know what to say.

Dana's eyes stayed locked on me, fire simmering just under the surface.

"Are you going to answer me or just sit there, Antwon?" she pressed.

I sighed, dragging a hand down my face. "Dana, I don't think Eddie's trying to drag you in. If anything, I think—"

"You think what?" Her voice cracked sharply. "That this is all a coincidence? That he just happened to hire the man I'm with; the man I finally decided to give another chance?"

"Dana—"

"No," she cut me off, rising from the bed. "You should've told me the moment he walked into your office. Instead, you've been sitting at dinner with me, lying in bed with me, all while carrying him between your shoulders."

I stood too, closing the space. "I didn't want to hurt you—"

"Hurt me?!" she threw back, incredulous. "Keeping secrets hurts more than the truth ever could."

And then, in one sudden motion, she scooped up the file, flung it into the air. Papers rained down around us like a storm of broken promises. "You can keep your cases, Antwon. But I won't be collateral damage in another Eddie game."

Hayzel Greene

She grabbed her bag from the chair, slung it over her shoulder. Her eyes were glassy, her jaw trembling—but she didn't break.

"Dana—wait."

She paused in the doorway but didn't turn.

"Please," I said, softer. "Don't let him win again by walking away from us."

Her breath hitched. But she shook her head and stepped out, the sound of the door slamming echoing through the house.

I stood there, surrounded by scattered papers and silence, a single thought cutting deeper than the rest:

I was losing her. Not to Eddie this time. But to my own damn silence.

Beyond the Dare

Chapter 25 – Dana

The drive home felt longer than usual, headlights blurring as my chest kept tightening, loosening, tightening again. By the time I dropped my keys on the counter, I was shaking half from anger, half from shame.

I ignored the phone the first time it buzzed. And the second. And the third.

By the fourth, his name filled the screen, glowing in the dark. I flipped it face down on the couch. Let it vibrate against the cushion until it stilled.

You left without hearing me out.

I didn't want to hurt you.

Please call me back.

Dana, I'm sorry.

The messages stacked one after another, desperate but careful, his lawyer's precision tucked even into his apologies. I read every one but answered none.

I sank onto the edge of my bed, head in my hands. The shame burned first. Snooping through his papers like I was a jealous teenager. But layered under that was anger. Weeks of half-smiles, half-conversations, blank stares at the dinner table. His body had been with me, but his mind. Somewhere else. With Eddie. With that case. With shadows I didn't ask to carry.

I curled on my side, blanket pulled over my head, willing sleep to come. It didn't. Instead, a memory slipped in, sharp and unwelcome: Eddie pressing a black box into my hands years ago, brushing it off like it was nothing. *"For you."*

I'd tucked it away in a crate when I left him, too bitter to throw out but too heavy to keep close. Tonight, something on my chest insisted I find it.

I dug through the back of the closet, hauling boxes into the light until I found it. Small. Black. Cold.

My hands shook as I opened it. Inside: a necklace I never wore, folded receipts, and beneath them—papers. Banking forms, routing numbers, a folder labeled with my name.

Holder: Dana M. _____

Depository: International Trust & Securities, Zurich.

Initial Balance: $250,000.

I flipped through, heart hammering. Deposits. Growth. A balance that no longer fits neatly into six figures.

Seven.

Millions. Sitting in my name.

I pressed the paper against my chest, breath shallow. The first wave was suspicion. *What kind of trap is this?* Then anger—Eddie using me, even when I didn't know it. But underneath both, something I couldn't ignore, temptation.

Hayzel Greene

I stared at the number until my vision became blurry. Who in their right mind walks away from this?

But was it even mine? Or was I just a name he used to hide his dirt?

I pulled my laptop into my lap and started digging. Hours blurred. I traced account activity, cross-checked statements, and searched for flags. Then, finally, a call—my voice steady, professional, when I asked the bank to "confirm ownership details."

And they did. Polite. Efficient. Clear.

The account was mine. Free and clear.

I ended the call with trembling hands, staring at the ceiling. For years I'd told myself Eddie had taken everything from me—my trust, my confidence, my worth. And now, by his own arrogance, he had left me the one thing I never expected: freedom.

The moral voice inside me whispered, *it's tainted. It's his.* But another voice—quieter, steadier—answered back: *No. He gave it to you. He hid it in your name. And now it's yours.*

I folded the papers neatly, set them on the nightstand, and lay back against the pillows.

The phone buzzed again. Antwon. His name glowed in the dark.

I didn't answer. Not yet.

Because tonight, I wasn't just the woman Eddie broke. I wasn't just the woman waiting for Antwon to tell me the truth.

Tonight, I was a woman staring at a future she never thought possible—one that suddenly, impossibly, belonged to me.

Chapter 26 – Antwon

The morning dragged. I sat at my desk, staring through the glass wall at the Akron skyline, but all I could see was her face when she stormed out. My phone buzzed every hour with another call I made, another text she ignored.

Dana, please pick up.

Talk to me. I didn't mean for it to happen like this.

You're the one thing that makes sense to me right now.

Nothing.

The silence pressed in; thicker than any cross-examination I'd ever faced. I'd beat prosecutors with nothing but a scrap of evidence and my voice, but I couldn't beat the distance in her silence.

The intercom snapped me out of it.
"Mr. Carrington, your 9:30 is waiting in the conference room."

Eddie.

My stomach turned. Of all mornings, it had to be this one. I sat there for a beat, gathering myself, staring at the file like it might burst into flames. Then I stood, grabbed my papers, and walked the longest ten feet of my life into that conference room.

He was already there. Leaning back in the chair like it was his throne, a smirk plastered across his face. The kind of smirk that said he knew exactly the wedge he was driving between me and Dana.

"Man of the hour," he said casually, folding his hands behind his head. "Didn't think I'd get the great Antwon Carrington himself."

I kept my voice even. "Let's keep this professional."

The tension between us filled the silence. Two men who knew exactly what the other meant to her, neither willing to blink.

And then the door opened.

Dana.

Not storming. Not fragile. Composed. Fierce. Flawless.

Blue pinstripe suit hugging her frame, blue stilettos clicking sharply against the tile, a blue-and-white Jimmy Choo dangling from her arm. Her hair was perfect; her posture was sharper than any blade. She didn't just walk into the room—she owned it.

She didn't sit at my side, didn't even look at me. She walked straight to the head of the table and sat down like it belonged to her. Her eyes cut into Eddie, voice cold enough to freeze stone.

"What the hell do you think you're doing here?"

Eddie's smirk twitched, cracking at the edges. "I'm here for the case. Nothing more, nothing less."

Her stomach clenched at the words, but she kept her face unreadable. *I already know, Eddie. I already found it. The account. The trail. The money.*

Eddie leaned forward, hands flat on the table now. "When I saw you two at that restaurant, I won't lie—I was jealous. But I also knew you weren't mine anymore. Then I got into trouble. And when I saw Carrington on TV, winning that Stokes case, and saw you in the background…" He exhaled. "I knew he was the one to get. Because the truth is, Subject X isn't just some ghost in the ledger. It's you, Dana. That account was always yours to control. And I can't access it without you. So, if he cares about you, he protects you. And if he protects you, he protects me."

For a second, silence strangled the room.

Dana's lips pressed tight. Inside, her mind screamed. *So that's it. He hired Antwon to get to me. Not because I was his weakness, but because I was his leverage. Because I had the key all along.*

But she didn't flinch.

She rose slowly, her voice shaking not from fear but fury. "You selfish bastard. You think dragging me into this circus is some kind of redemption? You think trusting him to clean up your mess makes you noble? Let me tell you something, Eddie—if anything happens to me because of this, I will handle you in a way you'll remember until your dying day."

Her chair screeched back. She grabbed her purse, heels clicking sharply against the floor, and stormed to the door. She paused only long enough to glare back at him.

"Stay away from me."

The door slammed so hard the glass rattled.

Eddie flinched. For once, he didn't have a damn word to say.

And all I could think, staring at the door she'd just disappeared through, was this:

If I didn't get her back... Eddie wouldn't be the one who broke her this time.

It would be me.

Chapter 27 – Antwon

The slam of the conference room door still rattled in my ears. For a second, I sat frozen, pulse hammering, her words echoing over Eddie's silence.

Selfish bastard.

Stay away from me.

Then I was on my feet, moving before logic caught up. I wasn't letting her leave like that—not after everything. Not with him still sitting in my damn office like a stain I couldn't scrub out.

Her heels clicked sharply down the hallway, faster than my stride, but I caught her just as the elevator doors slid open.

"Dana—wait."

She stepped into the elevator like she was trying to cut the air in half. Her hand stabbed the button so hard it rattled. Fury rolled off her in waves, sharp enough to slice.

Two interns tried to step in behind her. I threw an arm across the doorway. "Not this one."

They blinked, stammered, and backed away. The doors slid shut. Just us. The box hummed as it descended, numbers blinking, her perfume filling every inch of space.

"Let me go, Antwon," she hissed without looking at me, arms crossed like armor. Her eyes flashed wet but unbroken.

"No." My voice came out rougher than I meant. "Not like this."

The floor counter ticked down too fast, like I was about to lose her all over again. At the last second, I slammed my palm onto the red emergency stop. The jolt froze us mid-floor, silence buzzing like electricity.

She spun on me, eyes sparking. "What the hell are you doing?"

I didn't answer. Couldn't. *If this is the last time I touch her, let it burn.* All the words I'd been holding back burned out of me in one motion as I grabbed her face and crashed my mouth into hers.

It wasn't gentle. It wasn't planned. It was raw, desperate, the collision of rage and want that had been building for weeks. Her fists hit my chest once, hard. *Push him off. Push him away,* I saw her thinking—then her nails curled into my shoulders, dragging me closer even as she tried to shove me away.

"Stop it—" she gasped against my mouth.

"You don't want me to stop," I growled, biting her lower lip. "You're fire, Dana. That's the woman I've been chasing since Vegas."

"You make me crazy," she hissed, but her hips had already tilted into mine.

The elevator felt too small, too hot. Her back hit the wall with a thud. I pressed into her, caging her with my arms, my erection grinding against her thigh.

"I watched you tear into him out there," I whispered against her ear, my hands sliding under her blazer. "God, it turned me on. That mouth. That fire. You think I'm letting you storm off after that?"

She shuddered, eyes half-lidded now. "I hate you."

"No, you don't." I tugged her skirt up around her hips. "You want me. Right here. Right now."

Her breath tore out of her chest. "Do it then. Prove it."

I yanked her panties aside and shoved two fingers inside her, deep. She was already soaked. Her head hit the wall, a low moan slipping from her throat.

"Dripping for me," I muttered, curling my fingers until her thighs trembled around my wrist. "All that fire out there, and this—this is mine."

"Shut up and fuck me," she panted, nails clawing at my belt.

That undid me. My zipper hissed down, my dick springing free, thickly, and hard against her palm. She guided me to her entrance, eyes locked on mine, defiance and hunger swirling together.

"Take it," she whispered. "Take all of it."

I slammed into her with one hard, desperate stroke. Her scream filled the metal box, echoing off the walls. Her hands flew back to grip the rail as I filled her, stretched her, owned her.

"Fuck, Dana," I groaned, driving into her again, harder. "You're so tight I can't think."

She clamped her legs around my waist, heels digging into my ass, pulling me deeper. "Harder," she gasped. "I need it."

I pinned her wrists above her head, my body grinding hers into the wall, every thrust shaking the elevator. "This is us," I snarled. "Not him. Not the past. Us."

Her body seized around me, shuddering, the orgasm ripping through her so violently she sobbed against my shoulder, convulsing around me until I had no choice but to follow. I buried myself deep, spilling into her with a groan that rattled my bones.

We stayed locked together for a heartbeat, panting, slick, the air heavy with sex and sweat and something rawer than both. Her forehead pressed to mine, our breath mingling.

"You drive me crazy," I whispered, softer now, kissing her temple where minutes ago I'd been rough. "But I'll never let anyone else touch you. Not ever."

Her chest still heaved, but her hand came up to my cheek, trembling yet sure. "Then don't you dare let me go."

I released the emergency stop, the elevator humming back to life, carrying us down together, still tangled, the fight burned out, but the fire was still between us. *When the doors opened, nothing was fixed—but nothing would ever be the same.*

Chapter 28 – Dana

The office air still clung to me—stale coffee, paper, toner—and now sex. My body hummed with it, even as my heels clicked a furious rhythm down the hallway. My blazer sat crooked on my shoulders, my lipstick smudged, my thighs still trembling from what we'd just done.

God help me, I should've kept walking. Should've let that elevator close. But the second his mouth was on mine, all my fire turned combustible. Rage, lust, grief, every piece of me collided until there was nothing left but him.

And now?

Now I was walking out of Carrington & Associates with a body that still ached for him and a heart that didn't know which wound hurt worse: Eddie's shadow, or Antwon's silence.

The receptionist glanced up as I passed. Her gaze lingered too long. Did she know? Could she smell it on me? My cheeks burned as I stabbed the elevator button and didn't breathe until the doors sealed me in.

By the time I reached the lobby, my pulse had slowed, but not enough. The glass doors whooshed open, and Akron's evening air hit me sharp, cool. It should've sobered me. Instead, it carried his voice with it:

This is us. Not him. Not the past. Us.

I shoved the words away, but they clung like fingerprints on my skin.

Outside, traffic crawled, and horns blared. I kept my head high, crossing the street, fumbling my keys with hands that still shook. The car door shut around me, and for the first time since storming out of that conference room, I let my breath shatter.

Tears pricked but didn't fall. Instead, memory replayed like film reels: his growl in my ear, the rough way he held me, the soft way he kissed me after. He'd made me feel furious, reckless, alive. But Eddie's file still sat on his desk. Eddie's name was still between us. And no orgasm in the world could erase that.

I started the engine, headlights catching on the glass of his office building. Somewhere inside, he was probably straightening his tie, fixing his expression, preparing for his next meeting as if he hadn't just wrecked me against a desk.

And me? I was driving home to silence, to a bed that would still smell faintly of his cologne, to a choice I wasn't ready to make.

Because no matter how hard I tried to deny it, the truth was simple:
I didn't just want him.
I needed him.

So, whatever came next—in love or in court—would test whether we were strong enough to stand together.

Chapter 29 – Antwon

The courtroom buzzed like a hive—whispers, shuffling feet, the faint whir of cameras outside the doors. Reporters clutched notebooks, sketch artists' pencils flew, and the gallery strained forward for every sound. The air was thick with anticipation, smelling of paper, coffee, and nerves.

I adjusted my cufflinks, suit crisp and dark. My pulse was steady only because it had to be. Somewhere in the gallery, Dana sat—quiet, composed, her eyes locked on me. That single presence grounded me in chaos.

Eddie sat at the defense table, outwardly confident, but I knew better. His hands fidgeted under the table. The smirk he'd worn in my office was gone.

We'd already gutted majority of his witnesses on cross—contradictions laid bare like exposed wiring. Now comes the last push.

I rose. "The defense calls Mr. Ellison back to the stand."

The bailiff swore him in. The man's eyes darted as I approached. My questions came sharply as blades: dates, places, contradictions. Each answer tied tighter knots in the story Eddie's team had tried to spin.

Gasps rippled when I slid a new exhibit across. "Would you like to amend your previous testimony?"

He swallowed hard. "Yes."

The judge peered over her glasses. "Answer clearly, sir."

"Yes," he said louder.

I pressed. "So, the timeline your counsel presented—was it accurate?"

"No."

"Whose version is?"

"…Carrington's."

A low murmur rolled through the room. Even the sketch artist froze mid-line.

I turned to the jury, locking their eyes before closing my binder. "No further questions."

When it came time for closing arguments, I rose, feeling the weight of every ear in the room. I didn't give them theatrics. Just the truth, layered piece by piece, until the picture was undeniable: forged timelines, false statements, financial shells built to deceive. My voice stayed steady, relentless, threading it all together into a story that couldn't be unseen. Dana's eyes followed me the whole time.

The jury filed out. Hours stretched thin, every tick of the clock hammering my ribs. Dana slipped out once, returned with coffee, brushing her fingers against mine as she set it down. That small touch held me upright.

Finally: "All rise."

The jury filed back in, faces unreadable.

"Madam Foreperson," the judge said. "Have you reached a verdict?"

Hayzel Greene

"Yes, Your Honor."

The paper unfolded. The world stopped.

"On the charge of wire fraud, we find the defendant—Not Guilty."

The room erupted—gasps, cheers, angry murmurs, cameras firing. The judge banged the gavel. "Order! This is still a court of law!"

Eddie exhaled like a man surfacing from deep water. Relief flickered across his face, but so did something else, fear.

I stacked my files with deliberate precision, my jaw locked tight. He had not won. He had survived. And those are not the same.

When he rose, Eddie started to extend his hand—habit, arrogance, muscle memory. I took it, but instead of shaking, I pulled him an inch closer. Close enough for him to feel the steel in my grip.

"You're free now," I whispered, voice low and even. "But listen to me—Dana is off-limits. You so much as look her way again, you will answer to me. Understood?"

His throat worked. His eyes searched for a bluff, and he didn't find one. "Understood."

"Good," I said, tightening my grip once before letting go. "Because if you don't…fuck around and find out."

I released his hand, straightened my tie, and walked out without another glance.

The gallery parted like water. Dana rose from her seat, her hand sliding into mine as I passed. The cameras flashed, voices called, but for once I didn't hear a thing.

For the first time in weeks, the coil inside me loosened. This wasn't just a verdict. This was a line drawn.

Not guilty or not, Eddie would never touch what mattered most.

Epilogue I – Full Circle

Flashes popped across the courthouse steps like lightning. Reporters pressed in, microphones lunging forward, their voices a blur of questions—

Mr. Carrington, is this your biggest win?
Dana, how does it feel to be back in the spotlight?

None of it reached me. Not really.

What I felt was Antwon's hand in mine—warm, steady, sure—like an anchor in the noise. His body blocked me from the worst of the crowd, his voice low enough for only me.

"You, okay?" he murmured.

I lifted my chin. The old me would have ducked my head, shrunk back into the noise. Not today. "More than okay," I said, and I meant it.

Behind us, reporters swallowed Eddie. I didn't need to look to know Antwon had already handled him his words in the courtroom had cut sharper than any headline could:

You're free now. But Dana is off-limits. You so much as breathe her way again, you'll answer to me.

For the first time, Eddie understood. For the first time, I didn't feel like I was running from his shadow.

The cameras kept flashing, but they felt far away. What felt real was Antwon's palm against mine, our steps matching down the courthouse stairs. My heels clicked on the marble like punctuation, a rhythm that belonged to me now, not to anyone else's story.

The crowd parted. I leaned closer, my lips brushing Antwon's ear, my voice a private ribbon of sound inside the chaos.

"Vegas was a dare," I whispered. A confession. A truth.

He stopped, turned just enough so our eyes caught, his expression steady.

"But this?" I said, squeezing his hand tighter, a small smile tugging my lips. "This feels like forever."

And for the first time since Vegas, since Eddie, since all of it, I didn't just hope it.

I believed it.

Epilogue II – The Future

The living room was a sea of pastel balloons, gift bags stuffed with tissue paper, and laughter that carried through the walls. Dana sat in the center, glowing in a soft cream dress that skimmed her round belly, her hand moving absentmindedly over the curve every time the baby shifted.

Sam was the loudest, of course, making a game out of every open gift. "Diaper Genie? Girl, I don't even trust myself with that many buttons!"

Lani snapped photos on her phone, already narrating for the group chat. "Don't worry, baby—Auntie Lani's got you covered. You'll never run out of sneakers before your first birthday."

Dana's laugh rang out, full and unguarded. This was her circle—the women who'd seen her broken, carried her through Eddie, and now stood around her as she built something whole.

Dre strolled in fashionably late, shades still on indoors. He handed over a small bag and dropped onto the couch like he owned the room. "Before y'all start, yes—it's another pair of Jordans. Baby gotta come out fresh."

"Lord," Sam groaned, "you trying to turn the kid into a sneakerhead before it can crawl?"

Danielle swatted Dre's arm as she leaned over to peek in the bag. "You are ridiculous."

Dre grinned, tilting his head just enough to catch her eyes. "Yeah, but you like it, though."

The room erupted—Sam hollering, Lani choking on her mimosa, Dana covering her mouth with a wide-eyed laugh. Danielle rolled her eyes, but the hint of a smile gave her away.

Antwon crossed the room, then, pressing a kiss to Dana's temple before kneeling to touch her belly. "How's my little champ doing in there?"

The baby kicked, right on cue, and Dana's eyes softened. "Ready to meet you."

Antwon's gaze lifted to hers—steady, full, forever. And surrounded by the people who'd been there from the beginning, Dana felt it down to her bones.

The laughter swelled, the baby kicked, and for the first time, the story felt less like an ending—and more like a beginning.

Sometimes, forever starts with a single dare. Ours had turned into everything.

About the Author – Hayzel Greene

Hayzel Greene is a storyteller, screenwriter, and author who thrives at the crossroads of romance, drama, and raw emotion. She is the voice behind The HG Collection—a growing catalog of fiction that captures real, unapologetic stories about love, struggle, and resilience.

With three self-published short story books, multiple podcast-style audio series, and her debut film project *Flower: A Dope Girl's Story*, Hayzel continues to build worlds that resonate with both heart and grit. Her work blends vivid characters with layered conflicts, often rooted in themes of second chances, redemption, and the complexity of desire.

Beyond the Dare marks her return to one of her earliest short stories, expanding it into a powerful tale of love tested by time, secrets, and redemption. It is proof of her favorite motto: *"Stories linger long after the last page."*

"She writes for those who dare to love again."

Other Works by Hayzel Greene

Coming Soon

- **Flower: A Dope Girl's Story** *(Film)*
- **My Brother's Keeper**
- **Caught In the Setup**
- **The Consultant's Truth**
- **Nightstand Chronicles**
- **Dani's Tale II**
- **D'Motivation**
- **Loving Taye'Viare**

Also published by Hayzel Greene

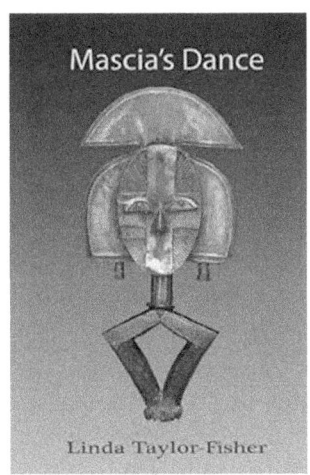

www.ingramcontent.com/pod-product-compliance
Lightning Source LLC
Chambersburg PA
CBHW051345020726
47501CB00007B/2284